FOUR
GEEZERS
VISIT
CROMER

MIKE TURVIL

Dedicated to all the old timers who have still got the spirit to get out there and enjoy life to the full. Forever young at heart

Contents

1

FOUR OLD BLOKES

"I can't wait for next weekend," John said to his companion. He and George were sitting perched on a pair of stools at the bar in the lounge of the Nag's Head. It was a damp Tuesday evening in late August and they both held a pint of beer, which they were savouring in the way that only real ale enthusiasts seem to do.

"Yes," said George. "It seems to have taken ages to get here, but it's only a few days away now."

They were referring to their weekend at Cromer, when they went with Fred and Tom to the picturesque Norfolk seaside town for a break. There they could forget all about their everyday lives, their wives where appropriate (John and Tom were both married) as well as the rest of their problems and simply concentrate on enjoying themselves.

This would be their fifth annual Cromer trip and what had started off as an overnight stay to take in the End of the Pier Show, had developed into a three day weekend which incorporated as many daft activities as they could possibly think of. It was their 'boys' weekend', not that any of them could now be called boys. Their ages ranged from early to late sixties and all of them had stopped working some years previously.

Fred was the eldest of the group and had once been in the Royal Navy, where he had risen to the dizzy heights of Chief Petty Officer, having enlisted as an apprentice at the tender age of sixteen years. He had never got married, because of all the time he had spent at sea, and was now very set in his ways and a confirmed older bachelor.

His service days were long behind him, but all those years of rigid discipline had left their mark. Fred saw himself as an organiser and it was his duty to make sure that the others kept to a properly planned schedule for the weekend. It would be no good suggesting to him that a Saturday activity be moved to Sunday, if Fred's timetable of events said it was to take place on the Saturday.

The others all accepted that this was what Fred was like, but that didn't stop them making fun of him. They often used to give him mock salutes whenever his back was turned. They did however realise that unless someone kept things under control to a certain extent, their fun weekend could quickly turn into a complete shambles and they wouldn't get half as much enjoyment out of it.

George had spent his working life in advertising, but his only real claim to fame was that he had come up with the tag line for a well known brand of toothpaste. The fact that George had to have all his teeth extracted at the age of forty-five and now wore false ones was rather ironic in the circumstances. It also didn't say a lot for the brand of toothpaste he had been using.

He often yearned to be able to bite into a nice crisp apple again, but couldn't risk his top plate getting embedded and the embarrassment this would cause. Before he went to bed each night, he would remove his false choppers and drop them into a glass by his bedside, where they would happily fizz away in a solution of Steradent until the morning.

George had been married once, but that was a very long time ago and had ended in divorce. Now he was a contented single man, who enjoyed nothing better than having a beer or two with his mates and a spot of gardening whenever he felt the inclination.

Tom was an eternal optimist and the dreamer of the group. He had spent his working life moving from job to job, as the grass always looked greener somewhere else to him. He had also tried several different careers, but never really found the one that suited him. Like Mr Micawber though, he always felt that his luck was about to change and was convinced that he would win the lottery one day.

He also spent a good deal of his time trying to chat up any women he met, as he considered himself to be quite a lady's man. This didn't go down too well with his wife, but she had learnt to live with it over the years. She really hoped that he was right about winning the lottery, as they would then be able to afford a divorce and she could start her life afresh with the huge settlement she would receive. It would also mean that she would no longer have to listen to him going on endlessly about his pipe dreams and wouldn't have to put up with all his womanising.

The last of the group was John. He was also married and had a grown-up son with a successful career. He was the only one of the group with any grandchildren, who he loved to bits and spoilt rotten. Nothing pleased him more than when they came to see him and he could bounce them on his knee. He really loved being called 'grandad'.

John had worked his way up to a senior managerial position in an international engineering company prior to retiring and had more money than the rest of the group put together. He and his wife lived in a large house on a private estate, but he wasn't at all snobbish about his wealth. He was proud of what he had managed to achieve through a lifetime of hard work and was always generous, if any of his friends were in need of assistance.

"So what do you think of this beer?" George asked. "I think I preferred the guest ale they had on last week." He was staring longingly at the bag of peanuts John was happily chomping his way through, but knew that they would play hell with his false teeth if he dared try any of them.

"It's not too bad," John replied, "but it's a bit lacking in body."

"Which body's that?" enquired Tom, who had just walked into the pub and joined them. He glanced around the bar, in case John had been referring to some attractive young lady, but was disappointed to see that there weren't any about.

"He is talking about the beer," George told him. "Don't you ever stop thinking about women?"

"Not while I've still got lead in my pencil," Tom replied with a laugh.

"Here's Fred," said John, as the ex-navy man came in from the other bar. "He's carrying some sheets of paper and I bet you anything you like that it's his carefully prepared itinerary for our Cromer weekend."

"Hi guys," Fred greeted them. "I was waiting for you in the other bar. I didn't realise that you were all in here."

"I've only just walked in myself," Tom told him. "I was just about to order another round. What does anybody want?"

After the drinks had been purchased, the four of them crossed the bar to a spare table and sat down. Fred placed the sheets of paper he had been carrying on the tabletop.

"I'm sure you're just dying to hear what I've got planned for this weekend," he said.

The others slowly but dutifully nodded their heads in agreement and Fred began to outline his schedule for their fifth Cromer weekend.

Tom was the only one of the group who didn't have a driving licence, so the others all took turns as to whose car they used. This year was John's turn, which meant that he would be spending a lot of time watching the rest of them drinking when he couldn't. He groaned when this was pointed out to him but it was only fair, as George had driven last year and Fred had done the driving the year before.

The others liked it when John was the nominated driver, because his car was a big comfortable Jaguar and there was room for the three of them to sit together on the back seat. John had to sit on his own at the front, which gave the appearance that he was their chauffeur. He refused to wear the peaked cap they had bought him for a laugh though.

They stopped smiling when he told them that he was thinking of using his wife's mini this year and that they would all have to squeeze into that, together with the luggage. He had said it with such a straight face that it took some time before they realised he was winding them up. By the time they cottoned on, he had already been treated to another pint of beer, a packet of crisps and a bag of peanuts.

"The weather forecast for this weekend is pretty good," Fred told them, "so it shouldn't interfere with any of the sporting events we've got planned."

The sporting events in question never include anything too energetic, as this would not be appropriate for four older gentlemen. The term 'sport' is used only in its loosest sense, as petanque amongst the rock pools on the beach (using brightly coloured plastic boules) and crazy golf on a scrubby patch of council land do not normally find their way into the Olympic Games. The Olympics also don't include pool competitions, unless they are of the aquatic sort, or 'Owzthat', a pocket cricket game as played by schoolboys years ago (for an explanation of the game of 'Owzthat', please refer to Page 47).

Eighteen holes on a pitch and putt course could arguably be considered by some to be sport, but not when two of the players know next to nothing about golf and the other two consider themselves to be seasoned experts. The team selection remains unchanged from year to year, but matches are invariably followed by a hole by hole analysis of what went wrong where and why it did. Excuses such as: "I would have made that putt on the seventh, if only that leaf hadn't got in the way," have sometimes been used to excuse a poor putting shot.

The less sporting activities include the End of the Pier Show. Cromer is now the only pier in the world where this continues to be an annual event and it is extremely well supported. A visit to the North Norfolk Railway for their annual steam gala is always included as well, providing it is taking place on the same weekend, and the Sunday lunchtime pint at the King's Arms at Reepham, listening to a live traditional jazz band for a couple of hours, is something that cannot be missed. It is a bit hard on the nominated driver, who can't relax and have a few beers because he still has to get them all home, but the music makes this worth suffering.

The lifting of heavy glasses of beer has been deliberately left out of the list of events (although all four of our heroes have considerable experience) but a good deal of time is always spent practising the art of glass lifting in various alehouses around the Cromer area.

The other thing that does need to be mentioned is the need for life supporting food. The hotel the boys stay at serves a very hearty full English breakfast, which provides a good start each morning. Cromer also has innumerable seafood takeaway places, various fish and chip shops and several restaurants, which include Chinese, Indian and a large number of English ones. With all this food available to them throughout the day, there is never any question of our four older gentlemen fading away for lack of sustenance.

So, the scene is set. Cromer is just a few days away and Tom, George, Fred and John are all intent on making this one the best ever. After all, what could possibly go wrong? It is just four friends going away to enjoy a fun weekend.

2

THE WEEKEND STARTS HERE

The arrangement for the Friday morning was that everyone should meet at John's house by nine sharp. Fred was there several minutes early (as usual) and George arrived shortly afterwards. By nine fifteen, there was still no sign of Tom turning up.

"Where the hell is he then?" asked John, looking at all the other cases loaded in the boot of the Jaguar.

"It's just like him to be late," said Fred. "He knows how important it is to keep to the schedule and he is always the last one here."

"I will give him a call," said John, pulling out his mobile. He dialled the number of Tom's house and his wife Deidre answered.

"Hello John," she said. "Tom knows that he's late, but can't find his mobile phone. You know he won't go anywhere without it, but we've been searching everywhere and just can't find it."

"Well, why doesn't he call his mobile number from the house phone? He will then be able to hear it ringing and you should be able to find it."

"We hadn't thought of that," Deidre replied. "I'll hang up and do that right away."

John turned to the others and told them what Deirdre had said.

"Typical," was Fred's immediate reaction. "I had everything packed up and ready last night, so why couldn't he have done the same?"

"I did as well," said George. "I always do."

"Did you remember to pack that glass for your choppers?" Fred asked. He and the others could seldom resist making a joke about George having to wear false teeth.

"Of course I did," he replied. "I might not be as organised as you are Fred, but you never see me forgetting anything important."

Ten minutes later and Deidre dropped Tom off in her car. He looked flustered. "It was in the garden shed," he told them. "I took it up there with me last night and must have accidently left it on the bench."

"Can we get going now?" Fred asked with a little irritability. "It is nearly half past nine and we are already behind schedule."

Fifteen minutes into the journey and George (who never forgot anything important) realised that he hadn't remembered to bring his wallet. The Jaguar screeched to a halt, as John slammed on the brakes without bothering to glance in his rear view mirror.

The little old lady in the car behind them only just about managed to stop in time. John jumped out of his car and ran back to apologise to her. He was rather startled to hear what she called him. It was definitely not the sort of language he expected to hear from a sweet little old lady.

Having returned to George's house for his wallet, they set off again with Fred tut-tutting in the back of the car. They were now an hour behind schedule and if things carried on the way they were going, all his carefully prepared plans for the day were going to get messed up.

Prostate troubles do affect some older men and among them, one has to include Tom. His prostate gland was giving him problems, which meant that when he had to go, he had to go. They had only travelled as far as Swaffham, when he announced that he needed to find a toilet rather urgently.

Swaffham is quite a large market town, with a lot of shops and several pubs. It is the sort of place where you might expect to find any number of public toilets, but there you would be mistaken. There is actually only one in the town centre and it is located near to where the market is held. John parked the car as close as he could and Tom leapt out and hobbled towards the loo. By now he was desperate and when he saw the sign on the gate, announcing that the toilets were temporarily closed for redecoration, his agitation level went off the scale. He returned to the car, as fast as his delicate condition would allow, and told the others.

"There is a big supermarket just off the Castle Acre Road," Fred told him. "You will just have to hang on until we get there."

"I will try," Tom responded, "but can't make any promises."

"You had better not pee on the back seat of my Jaguar," John warned him.

They made it in time and a few minutes later, a much relieved Tom returned to the car. "Sorry about that chaps," he said, but then noticed that George was missing.

"He's gone to get a new battery for his alarm clock," Fred informed him. "Something else he forgot to bring. I will be surprised if we ever get to Cromer at this rate."

Inside the store, George was having problems with the lady at the checkout. "This coupon was only valid until yesterday," she was telling him, "so you can't use it to get a discount on those batteries."

The pack of batteries only cost £3.75, but rather than fish around in his pocket for change, George gave her his credit card to speed things along. The machine at the till rejected it. "My machine is playing up today," he was told. "Don't you carry any cash?"

The problem with paying for the batteries was finally overcome and George returned to the car, where the others were beginning to wonder what had become of him. They set off again. Cromer was now about forty miles away, but they intended to stop off at Sherringham railway station to have a look at all the old steam locomotives they knew would be standing at the platform.

The boys were mostly old enough to remember the golden age of steam, so seeing real trains again was something of a nostalgic experience for them. They knew they might have difficulty parking though, as the Friday market takes place in the town's main car park. This reduces the number of available parking places on a day when the town is extra busy to begin with, because of all the additional visitors who have come to see the trains.

It would be a while yet before they needed to face that problem however; as fate had decreed that they were going to get delayed even further.

They were still a good twenty five miles from Sherringham when they came up behind a long line of other vehicles, that was hardly moving at all. "What's going on here?" asked Fred.

A policeman on a motorbike shot past them and continued to pass all the other cars in the queue. "Must be an accident or something," John observed. "Hopefully, it shouldn't delay us for too long."

Half an hour or so later, they reached the front of the line, where the police motorcyclist was busy directing traffic around a stationary monster truck. He lifted up his hand to get them to stop them and motioned to the traffic coming the other way to start moving. He then walked over to John's open window and spoke to him.

"There is a big country fair on at Fakenham this weekend," he said, "and that monster truck is on its way there. Unfortunately, it got a puncture and the driver is waiting for another tyre to be brought out to him. It should be on the back of a transporter and not on the road at all, but the prat who is driving it wanted to arrive at the fairground in style."

The boys looked across at the truck with its five and a half feet diameter tyres. They were so huge that they towered above John's Jaguar and even the tread pattern was at least four inches deep. "How on earth can you get a puncture in tyres that size?" Tom asked, with some incredulity.

"Maybe he ran over a hedgehog," George suggested with a grin.

After passing the monster truck, they continued on their way towards Fakenham, but only managed to travel another three miles before they saw yet another policeman by the side of the road. He waved at them to stop and walked over to the car.

"There is an escaped chimpanzee in this area," he told them, "so I'm warning drivers to watch out for it and to keep their windows shut."

"Where did it escape from?" asked John in disbelief.

"From the circus on the green," the policeman told him. "There is a big show there this weekend and the circus is part of it. There is also a fairground and lots of other attractions, like traction engines, vintage cars, monster trucks and the like."

"Is this chimpanzee dangerous?" asked George.

He wasn't all that keen on wild animals.

"I shouldn't think so," the policeman replied, "but you can never tell. I certainly wouldn't want to go anywhere near it if I was eating a banana."

"Or drinking a cup of tea?" Tom suggested. "I seem to remember that chimps like having tea parties!"

"Whatever," said the unamused officer and waved them on.

The chimp could of course have been anywhere at all, but just happened to be on sitting in the middle of the left hand lane of the A1065, half a mile ahead of them. John slowed right down as they approached the animal, as he didn't want to risk running it over. The chimp looked up as the car stopped, but then got up and ambled over towards it.

"Wind your window up," John yelled to Fred in the back. "I don't want the damn thing climbing into the car. Fred quickly pressed the button to close the open rear window.

The chimpanzee jumped up onto the bonnet and then stared through the windscreen at the slightly nervous passengers in the car.

"Put the windscreen wipers on," George suggested in John's ear. "It might frighten him off."

John followed George's advice and turned them on. The chimp watched them swishing backwards and forwards across the screen in utter fascination. It then made a grab for one of them.

"Hit it with your windscreen washers," George

further advised. "A lot of animals don't like water, so getting wet might make it jump off."

A lot of animals may not like getting splashed with water, but this particular chimpanzee clearly loved it. It was having the time of its life and was even trying to catch the spray in its mouth and drink it.

At that moment, a van pulled up and a man stepped out carrying a collar and lead. He walked over to the Jaguar and put the collar round the chimpanzee's neck. "Would you turn your bloody washers and wipers off, mate," he shouted at John. "I'm getting soaked here!"

John obliged and the man returned to his van with the chimpanzee. They all expected him to come back and say something to them, but he didn't. He just drove off immediately.

"There's gratitude for you," remarked John, "after we go to all the trouble of finding his escaped chimpanzee for him."

Half an hour or so later, they reached Sherringham and began scouring the car park for a vacant spot.

"Can't you squeeze it in there?" Fred asked, indicating an available parking spot that would have challenged the skills of a driver in a Smart car.

"This is a Jaguar, not a mini," John pointed out. "It needs a larger space than that. We will just have to keep looking until we find somewhere suitable."

As luck would have it, a huge people carrier drove away a few minutes later and John was able to claim its place. They all piled out of the car. "I'm just going to go over to the market to have a look round," John announced. "I will meet you all on the platform."

The others knew that this meant that John was going to head straight for the seafood stall, where he would buy himself a plate of whelks. John getting 'whelked-up' at every available opportunity was an accepted feature of their annual Cromer trip.

The others walked over to the station and as the platform bar was now open, promptly ordered three pints of beer. Despite all the mishaps of the morning, the world somehow seemed to look better as soon as they had a pint of beer in their hands and even Fred was beginning to show signs of being a bit more relaxed.

"There's a loo at the end of the platform Tom," he said, "just in case you get caught short again." Tom gave him a withering look and continued drinking his beer. John joined them a short while later. He had that satisfied expression on his face, which the others knew meant that his search for a plate of whelks had been successful and that he was fully 'whelked-up' for the moment.

"Were they up to standard?" Tom enquired.

"I don't know what you mean," John replied, which just made them all laugh even more.

3

WATCH WHERE YOU PUTT

After an hour or so of looking at the steam trains and another pint of beer for George and Fred, they decided that it was time to make a move and continue on towards Cromer. It was now after two in the afternoon, so they would be allowed to check-in to their hotel straight away. After which they would meet up outside and make a start on the first of the weekend's planned events. In the back of the car, Fred was busy shuffling his papers. They were well behind schedule, but not as far as he had feared they might be. It was beginning to look as if the rest of their first day of the weekend should work out all right after all.

It is not far from Sherringham to Cromer, so they reached their final destination fairly quickly. They collected their cases from the boot of the Jaguar and filed into the hotel. "We have pre-paid for the accommodation," Fred told the receptionist, "so all we need to pay for now are our breakfasts."

"Will you all be having a cooked breakfast each day, or will any of you want the continental one?" she asked.

"Eight cooked breakfasts please. One for each of us on both days," Tom said, "and I would like a room near one of the toilets if possible, please."

When they had originally begun using this hotel, they used to book two twin-bedded en-suite rooms. This was before they discovered how much their respective roommates snored. In recent years, Tom and John had taken to booking a single room each, with use of the bathroom down the hall. Fred and George continued to share a twin en-suite. They both snored as much as each other, but put up with this for the convenience of having a toilet in their room. It meant that they could avoid the dreaded march down the corridor in the middle of the night.

After they had paid for their breakfasts and carried the luggage up to their rooms (which in Tom's case meant to the top floor, as there was a toilet right next door to one of the rooms there) they met up again outside, ready to make a start on whatever was first on Fred's schedule.

They were now safely arrived in Cromer and raring to go and it was still relatively early on the Friday afternoon.

The boy's hotel was only a short distance from the town centre and pier and on the main coastal road which runs parallel to the cliffs. Immediately opposite their hotel is the municipal putting green, next door to the bowls club. These facilities are separated by a long low wooden building, which houses the clubhouse for the bowlers and the little hut where people hire the equipment needed for the putting green. The path which divides the putting green in two runs from the pavement to the edge of the cliffs and is less than fifty yards long. What the course lacks in width however is made up for by its length, as it is over two hundred yards long. There are five tiered playing areas, the first of which is for the first and eighteenth holes.

To reach the second level, players need to descend down a short set of steps and cross the dividing path, before ascending another set of steps to reach the next part of the course. From here onwards, the ground slopes off in every direction and there are little rockery flowerbeds positioned in between the holes, to add a bit of colour and additional hazards.

Another set of steps separates the second and third levels, while yet another set separates the third and fourth. There are no steps between the fourth and fifth tiers (the halfway point) as whoever designed the course cunningly decided that players would need to putt up and down the thirty degree bank positioned at this point.

The course is not particularly challenging, apart from the problem of trying to judge the right speed to send your ball either up or down the bank, and the condition of the grass surface itself is quite good, considering that it is only maintained by a veteran council worker with his lawn mower.

A round on the putting green is an obligatory event for the boy's Cromer weekend, so this Friday afternoon saw them strolling towards the hut where they would need to pay to do so. It was to be a team event and George and John (as the seasoned golfers) were on opposing teams. Fred played with George and Tom had John as his partner. Despite the fact that all four of them had putting clubs and a number seven iron in the boot of the Jaguar (which they would use on the pitch and putt course in a later competition) they hired what passed for putters on a council putting green and were each given different brightly coloured balls.

John teed off and his red ball stopped less than a yard from the first hole. "Good shot," shouted Tom. "We are putting them under pressure right from the start."

Fred went next, but his blue ball only travelled three quarters of the way to the hole. Having seen this, Tom decided that he would need to hit his ball harder than Fred had, so gave it an almighty whack. By the merest chance, it collided with Fred's ball and stopped dead. Fred's blue ball was shot forward by the impact and covered the rest of the distance to the hole, stopping just inches short.

"Why did you do that?" John protested to his partner. "Now you have given them the chance to halve the hole."

"All's fair in love and war," said George, as he prepared to take his first shot. His yellow ball went two yards past the hole before coming to rest.

John knew that even Fred was unlikely to miss a four inch putt and this unsettled him, as he attempted to putt his ball from thirty inches away. He missed the hole by a whisker and Fred and George both cheered. Fred managed to hole his ball and his team were in the lead. The game was not going the way John had hoped, but it was still early days and he wasn't going to let it upset him.

It seems to be a thing with people who play golf. They cannot resist the temptation of taking air shots with whatever club they happen to be holding at the time (and sometimes when they're not even holding a club at all). John was no exception. He began swishing his council putter around and having carefully sighted up on a spot two inches beyond his ball, launched into a driving shot that would have sent it a hundred and fifty yards, had he actually been aiming for the ball.

The wasp that flew into John's face at the beginning of his stroke did so quite innocently and there was no malice aforethought. It was however enough to cause John to jump backwards in the middle of his swing. His putter sliced an arc through the air and made very positive contact with his ball on the ground, which took off at a hundred miles an hour in the direction of the low wooden building.

The league match on the bowls green next door was at a very crucial stage. It was the final end and the last team player for the Sherringham District League was about to have his turn. All he needed to do for his side to win was to position his bowl within six inches of the jack. Having carefully checked his grip, he stepped onto the mat and drew back his arm, before swinging it forward and releasing the bowl. He judged it to perfection and knew straight away that this was going to be the winning shot and that his side would be victorious.

At that moment, a bright red golf ball sailed over the clubhouse and landed right in the middle of the head, hitting the jack. The force of the collision was enough to move it twelve inches and its new position was now much closer to a completely different bowl - one that had been rolled by a member of the Cromer team. The final bowl sent down the rink was indeed on target, or would have been had the jack still been in the same place. As it was, it was too far away to count, which meant that Sherringham had failed in their attempt to secure the end and win the match.

Pandemonium broke out as the Sherringham team members began arguing vociferously about what had just happened. The final bowler went absolutely berserk and was jumping up and down on the spot and screaming out about being robbed. Needless to say, the Cromer team didn't see the incident in quite the same way and their captain was insisting that it could only be viewed as an unforeseen accident, a 'force majeure' for which no one could be blamed.

"It's hardly an act of God," the Sherringham team captain complained, "when some prat on the putting green next door knocks a ball into the middle of the head during an important league game!"

"But I'm sure they didn't intend to interfere with the match," the Cromer captain responded.

It was at that moment that John walked in through the gate and politely asked if he could have his ball back. He wasn't quite expecting the response he received. This was the second time today that he had been sworn at and he was getting rather fed up with people keep having a go at him. He didn't know why everyone seemed to be so angry and was even more surprised when one of the team members picked up his golf ball and hurled it over the cliff and into the sea.

By now, the club secretary had gone and got his copy of the rule book from the clubhouse and was busy thumbing through the pages. He was hoping to find some ruling in it about what should be done in such circumstances. John decided that his presence wasn't helping the situation and that he had best leave them to it. He went back out through the gate to rejoin his colleagues on the putting green, but now he didn't have a ball to play with.

The lady at the hire shop hadn't seen John's magnificent drive, so didn't know what had become of his ball. She did however know the rules as far as the putting green was concerned. She insisted that he would have to pay fifty pence for the lost ball, before she would give him another one. There was no convincing her otherwise, so

John had no choice but to pay for a replacement ball. This then created a further problem, because she had given him a yellow ball, which was the same colour as the one George was playing.

The game continued after everything had been sorted out and George and Fred eventually managed to win by two holes. John immediately claimed that his team had only lost because he hadn't been able to focus on the game, following the incident with the members of the bowls club. George and Fred weren't at all sympathetic, as John and Tom had won the last three years running. They were absolutely delighted with the result.

"I need a drink," John told them, after they had handed back their rental equipment. "Let's walk into town and have a pint at the Old Boot. You lot have got a head start on me, so it's time I had a beer."

The Old Boot Hotel is a very popular watering hole for both locals and visitors alike and has a good range of beers and an enclosed outside courtyard for when the weather is warm and sunny. John was so intent on the thought of getting a pint of beer down his neck, that he actually walked straight passed a seafood stall without even bothering to look at the whelks on offer. He did however become a bit happier after he had got his pint of beer and the conversation turned to discussing the forthcoming sporting challenges.

"After we've had a pint here," Fred said, "we could always go over to the community club and begin playing some of the pool matches. We've got the singles and doubles to play, so the sooner we can make a start on them the better."

"Not now Fred," Tom suggested. "We have all day tomorrow and Sunday morning, so there is no great rush. The others agreed and Fred was outvoted. He didn't bother to argue, but knew that it meant that he would have to jigger around with his planned schedule.

"I need to collect the tickets for tomorrow night's show from the booking office on the pier," George told them, "so I'll wander over there now and meet you guys back here." He got up and left.

One of the regular events for the Cromer weekend is to try and forecast the results of six of the Saturday football matches. It is a pay to play event (a pound each) and the person with the most correct forecasts scoops the pot. No one had ever managed to pick all six correct results yet, which would have meant actually winning money from the bookie as well, but Tom was going to try out his new system this year. He was convinced that this would make him the winner, even though he knew next to nothing about football.

"Someone also needs to pick up some betting slips from the bookies," Tom said, "so I will do that now." He then got up to go as well, leaving just Fred and John in the pub. They decided to order another pint.

4

FISH AND CHIPS CAN KILL YOU

It seemed to be George's day for problems, because the woman at the theatre office couldn't find any record of him having made a booking.

"I ordered them on-line a month ago," he said. "You must have something there to show that."

"Well, your name isn't on the booking list," was her reply. "What seats were you trying to get?"

"My booking was for Row E, seats 14, 15, 16 and 17. Do your records show them as reserved?"

The woman consulted her list again and confirmed that those four seats had been pre-booked, but under the name of Mr Paypal.

"I used PayPal when I made the booking," George told her, "but my name is Wilson, George Wilson."

She went back to her list again, but still couldn't find any trace of his name. "The only thing I can suggest," she said, "is that you and your friends turn up for tomorrow night's performance and if

Mr Paypal hasn't claimed his tickets by the time the show is about to start then I will let you have his, but you will still have to pay for them."

"I'm not going to pay twice," George said huffily. "I think I have my confirmation of the booking back at the hotel, so I will bring that here in the morning and hopefully we can sort this all out then."

The woman shrugged as if to say it was up to him and then looked at the man queuing behind George. "Can I help you?" she asked. George gave up and walked away. He was shaking his head in disbelief.

Tom was busy trying to chat up the pretty girl at the counter in the bookies. "So what time do you get off?" he asked. "I'm here for the whole weekend and would love to see more of you."

She walked out from behind the counter and stood there facing Tom with her hands on her hips. "Now you've seen all of me," she said. "So are you going to place a bet or not, because I'm very busy?"

Tom was a bit flustered and muttered something about placing a bet later. He clearly wasn't getting anywhere, so decided that a strategic exit was in order. He headed for the door.

"Bloomin' cheek," the girl said after he had left the shop. "What is it about this place that seems to attract all the dirty old men in the area?"

When George and Tom returned to the Old Boot, George explained about the difficulties with the tickets and how he was hoping to sort it out the following morning. Tom didn't bother to say anything about his failed attempt to chat up the young lady in the bookies. He was only glad that the others hadn't been there to see it.

The four of them then began to pick their teams for the Saturday matches. There are many ways of doing this, but John's method was to just pick six games at random and then alternate between home, away and draws in a pretty pattern on his betting slip. Tom new scientific method was to only select matches where the result was almost a foregone conclusion. The odds for these matches only produced very low returns, so even if he did successfully pick all six, his winnings probably wouldn't be enough to cover a round of drinks.

Fred and George are both very keen football fans, so there was much discussion between the pair of them as to the likely outcome of various different matches. They were the ones who took longest to complete their betting slips and each was convinced that they had correctly predicted the results of the games they had selected.

Fred took charge of the completed betting slips and would drop them off at the bookies in the morning. The afternoon was well advanced by now and they decided to go for a stroll round the town. This wasn't to be their annual shopping trip (as they would do that tomorrow) but they hadn't been to the Lifeboat Museum in a while and the place was always worth visiting. There was also the point that it was on the same level as the beach, so the climb back up to the town would give them an appetite.

They used to go to Shirley's Pie and Mash Shop for their Friday evening meal, where they had a choice of six different sorts of traditional meat pies (and a couple of vegetarian ones), several mash and potato options and various gravies, including Shirley's own special liquor sauce. The cost for this treat was only £9.00 and not only was it great value for money, but it was also highly enjoyable and very satisfying.

Unfortunately, Shirley's had to close because the restaurant just wasn't big enough to cater for the demand. The boys were upset about this, as they used to look forward to their Friday evening pie and mash at Cromer. What it also meant however, was that they needed to find somewhere else to eat.

As mentioned previously, there are a lot of fish and chip shops in Cromer, as evidenced by the fact that at any time of the day (and often well into the night) you can always see tourists wandering around eating fish and chips out of plastic containers.

Even with so many other fish and chip shops being open and serving, it is interesting to note that there is always a queue outside Sally Anne's Fish Bar and Restaurant. It is there from well before the place opens in the morning and continues throughout the day. The boys had long since decided that there had to be a good reason for this, so whenever they decided to dine on fish and chips, they always went to see Sally Anne.

Sally Anne's website says that hers is the best fish and chip shop in Cromer and the only one with an award from the Federation of Fish Friars. This could just be a spelling mistake, or may have something to do with fish being good for the 'sole'. Either way, when the boys all agreed that they should finish off the day with a fish and chips supper; there was no argument about where to go for it. They walked the short distance up the street to Sally Anne's establishment and joined the queue outside. By now, it was just after eight in the evening.

"Most of these people here are waiting to order a takeaway," Fred observed. "Let's go through that other door to the restaurant and see if they can find us a table."

They bypassed the queue and entered the restaurant. Tom immediately began looking around, as he always like to know where the nearest toilet was in case he suddenly needed to go. There was no problem with them finding a table for four and having taken their seats, they all began to study the menu.

"I'm feeling quite peckish after all that beer," George said, "so I think I will go for the large cod and chips."

"I found a bone in mine the last time I ordered that," John told him. "I don't think it matters how careful they are, it is virtually impossible to remove every single bone from big chunks of fish."

"Well, that was just your bad luck," George replied. "I'm sure mine will be fine."

They all plaiced their orders (possibly another spelling mistake?) and waited for their meals to arrive. Sally Anne's has a drinks license, so they all ordered another beer to help the fish and chips go down.

Their meals turned up fairly quickly, considering how busy the place was and how many meals were being served simultaneously and they began to tuck in with relish, after having liberally dosed their fish and chips with plenty of salt and vinegar.

It was inevitable that there would be a bone in George's piece of cod, but it was rather unfortunate that he didn't notice this until it was half way down his throat.

He suddenly stopped eating and became very quiet, but then began to turn red in the face. He was struggling for air, but it took a moment or two for the others to notice. By this time, George had stood up and clearly had a serious problem.

"He's swallowed a bone and it's got stuck in his throat," John shouted. "What should we do?"

They all took turns to slap him hard on the back, but this didn't do any good and George was now close to the point of passing out.

"You need to do the Heimlech manoeuvre," another diner shouted across at them. "Do any of you know how to do it?"

The other three exchanged puzzled glances, but then a waitress rushed over. She grabbed George from behind and having positioned her fists together beneath his ribcage at the front, she suddenly jerked them both backwards. George's top plate shot out of his mouth and landed at the feet of the woman on the next table. She promptly fainted. The waitress then continued to pummel George's stomach with a ferocity the others found alarming.

What she was doing finally worked and the chunk of fish with a bone in it popped out of George's mouth and flew across the restaurant. It splashed down in a cup of tea a few tables away, much to the surprise of the man holding the cup. George stood there gasping in air, as his face slowly returned to a more normal colour. He had thought he was about to die and was shaking uncontrollably.

"Wow!" said Tom. "I've never seen anything like that before."

"It was a bloody good shot as well," exclaimed John.

Fred retrieved George's false teeth and they all helped him to sit down. He looked more normal once his teeth were back in his mouth and he slowly began to calm down. The others then thanked the waitress for her prompt action. She had done exactly what was necessary when they didn't have a clue what to do.

"It's in the standard training manual for staff who work in fish and chip restaurants," she explained.

After George had recovered, he thanked the waitress himself. "I don't know what to say," He told her. "But for you I might have died there, as this lot were no use at all."

"Well, you certainly added a bit of excitement to our Cromer weekend," Fred said, trying to make light of the situation. They had all been seriously shocked by what had just happened.

The rest of their meal was eaten rather slowly, with all of them carefully examining each forkful of food before putting it in their mouths. After they had finished, George gave his life-saving waitress a ten pound tip, which made her blush.

As they left the restaurant, he turned to the others and said, "This has been a very eventful day and I'm quite glad it's nearly over. I don't think I could cope with anything else going wrong. I suggest we have another beer somewhere and then go back to the hotel. Tomorrow is another day and things can only improve."

"At least your team won the putting competition," John commented, "but I think you are right. We've all had about enough excitement for one day, so a quick beer to round off the evening and then we should call it a night."

With that, they began to walk back, stopping off at the Imperial Hotel on the way.

The Imperial is a large luxury establishment, but it is a bit expensive to stay there. John was the only one who could afford their room rates and although he had offered make up the difference for the others, they didn't want to take advantage of his generosity to that extent. This didn't stop them drinking there from time to time though and there was always the attraction of the young foreign barmaid. She was a very pretty girl and Tom had tried every line he could think of on her, but without success. She just smiled sweetly at him and pretended that she couldn't understand what he was saying.

After a nightcap at the Imperial, they returned to their own hotel, checking to see if the bar was open on their way in. In all the years that they had been using this hotel, they had never actually seen the bar open. Its opening hours were clearly one of life's mysteries.

"Shut again!" said Tom. "What a surprise!"

With that, they all wished each other good night and retired to their respective rooms for an early night.

5

VISITORS IN THE NIGHT

Unbeknown to the four of them, as they snored the night away in blissful ignorance, a gang of thieves had spotted John's Jaguar in the hotel car park during the afternoon and intended to return to it in the very early hours of the morning. They weren't at all interested in stealing the car, but the wheels and tyres were something they could dispose of very easily and would fetch a good price.

Cromer is not the sort of place where there is a high level of criminal activity, but these thieves were visiting from out of town and were spending their time in Cromer on the lookout for any opportunities to make some quick money.

This hotel operates a system at breakfast time and the very first time the boys stayed there, they fell foul of the system and caused all sorts of mayhem. John had been the first one down for breakfast on that occasion and paid scant attention to the fact that all the tables had little numbered plaques on them. After all, it is quite common to see numbered tables in restaurants, as it enables the servers to know where the food needs to be delivered.

Fred joined him as he was about to order, so the waiter took both their orders and disappeared into the kitchen. The problem came later, when the restaurant manager (who also happened to be the hotel manager) delivered their food to the table. As he put down their plates, he seemed to be somewhat perplexed. John and Fred didn't take any notice and immediately started eating their breakfasts.

"What rooms are you two in?" the manager almost demanded of them. When they told him that they were sharing room 11, he seemed to get rather upset.

"Is there a problem?" Fred asked.

"You are sitting at the wrong table," the man told him. "You will have to move."

"We just picked a free table," John explained. "How were we supposed to know that it's the wrong one?"

"There are four of you altogether aren't there?" the manager continued. "You are staying in rooms 11 and 23, but this table is for room 17." John and Fred stared at him with confused expressions.

The manager pointed to the little plaque on the table, which had the number 17 on it. "If you look at that table over there," he said, pointing across the room, "you will see that the number plaques there are for rooms 11 and 23. That is where you should be sitting, not on number 17's table."

"Does it really make that much difference?" asked John.

"Of course it does," the manager told him. "It is the system and everyone has to sit at their proper table."

As Tom and George arrived for their breakfasts, they were greeted by the sight of Fred and John carrying their plates across the room, with the manager fussing along behind them with two cups of coffee. They obviously didn't know what was going on, but tagged on to the little group anyway and joined Fred and John at the other table.

"This will be your table while you are staying here," the manager told them. "Please don't sit at any of the others." He then rushed back to the table where they had been sitting and began rearranging it in preparation for the arrival of whoever was staying in room 17.

Tom asked what this was all about, only to be told by John that he and Fred had committed a cardinal sin by sitting at the wrong table. They had totally messed up the carefully planned seating arrangements and had very probably completely spoiled the manager's day.

From that time onwards, whoever was first down for breakfast in the morning always made a point of checking the numbers on all the tables, to find out where they were meant to be sitting. They didn't want to risk upsetting the manager again.

They were all sitting at the right table on this

Saturday morning and were in the middle of their breakfasts when the manager entered from the kitchen. He walked straight over to where they were and stared at them.

"What have we done wrong now?" George asked the others.

"Does one of you own that Jaguar in the car park?" the manager enquired.

"It's mine," John answered him "Why? Is there a problem? Have I parked it in the wrong place or something?"

"Well, I suggest you might like to go and have a look at it," the manager replied. "I think you could call it a problem."

They all left the breakfasts where they were and trooped out into the car park. John's Jaguar was exactly where they had left it, but all four wheels were now missing and it was precariously balanced on little columns of bricks.

"I don't believe it!" John shouted in amazement. "Someone's stolen all my wheels."

"I've already called the police," the manager told him, "so they should be here any minute."

John and the others all glanced across at the CCTV camera, which they knew sat on a pole in the car park. The pole was still there, but the top of it was now adorned with a plastic red and white striped traffic cone. The thieves had obviously put it there to make sure their activities were not caught on film.

John's mouth dropped open in surprise and Fred

was heard to say, "That's a crafty thing to do!"

The arrival of the police was not marked by a squad car screeching to a halt with flashing lights, a blaring siren and coppers leaping out of it. There was actually just the one policeman and he peddled up on his push bike. He joined the group in the car park, looked at the Jaguar and then glanced across at the pole with the traffic cone on top.

"That's a shame," he said and then addressing the manager, asked whether the thieves had spotted the other camera.

"I think they might have missed that one," the manager told him.

All eyes turned to the manager, as he pointed out a second CCTV camera, high up on the wall under the eaves of the building. It was still there and there was nothing shielding its view. The thieves hadn't noticed this one.

"We had better have a look and see if it recorded anything useful," the policeman said.

A short while later and six men were standing in the manager's office, watching the playbacks from the two CCTV cameras. The manager had not wanted the boys to be there at all, but the policeman (who was a sergeant) had overruled him. The first screen suddenly blanked out, when the indicated time was just after three in the morning.

"That must be when they put the traffic cone on top of the pole," the policeman said, needlessly pointing out what was obvious to everyone.

All eyes focussed on the second screen, which

was displaying an image of the car park, with John's Jaguar sitting there quite happily with all four of its wheels still in place.

A van then pulled into the car park and a young man jumped out of the back with a trolley jack. He quickly positioned it under the middle of the back axle and began to pump the handle. The rear end of the Jaguar slowly lifted into the air. Two other men with bricks then got out of the van and slid under the back of the car to position their little supporting columns. All three then moved to the front end of the car and repeated the same procedure.

A fourth man appeared from the van and began undoing the wheel nuts on the rear offside wheel.

"My car had locking wheel nuts on all its wheels," John exclaimed. "How is he getting that one off so quickly?"

"They are obviously professionals and knew what they were doing." The policeman told him. "They must have brought along the right kind of spanner to deal with the locking wheel nuts on Jaguars."

It took just minutes for the thieves to remove all four wheels and the last useful image recorded was of them each rolling a wheel to the van, which then shot out of the car park. The camera had captured good images of the faces of two of the men and had recorded the van's registration number as well.

The policeman looked very satisfied with what he had just seen. "They made a big mistake when they didn't spot that other camera," he said, "but you have to admit, they were very efficient otherwise.

They'd probably make a very good pit team at any race track. "

"But what about my car?" John asked. "I can't drive it without any wheels and we need to go home tomorrow."

"I'm sure your insurance company will be able to arrange for them to be replaced," the policeman said, "particularly when they hear that we have the whole incident recorded on film."

"I'm going to go and ring them now," John said. He made a note of the policeman's name and number and rushed off to find somewhere to make the call.

The others watched him go and then Tom remarked about having missed breakfast.

The manager agreed that under the circumstances, he would serve the other three fresh breakfasts, even though the kitchen was now officially closed.

John joined them in the restaurant about half an hour later and told them that his insurance company were arranging for a new set of wheels and tyres to be delivered to the hotel and fitted to his car. "They are hoping to have it all sorted by lunchtime," he said, "so we might just as well get on with our planned activities for the day."

"Well, I need to visit the ticket office on the pier again," George mentioned, "so I will do that and then give you guys a ring to find out where you are."

"Okay," said John. "You do that. What is next on the itinerary Fred?"

Fred suddenly realised that he had left his list in the room, so immediately dashed off to get it. The others continued sitting at the table, all very conscious of the manager eyeing them from the kitchen door. All the other tables had already been reset for the lunchtime sitting, but theirs couldn't be done while they were still there. They decided to stay a bit longer, just to wind up the manager.

6

BEACH SHENANIGANS

From the cliff path opposite the hotel, it is possible to descend to the beach promenade by following a series of sloping concrete ramps, which zigzag down through three hairpin turns. Going down is very easy, but it can be quite a challenge when you have to walk back up. The council has thoughtfully provided little round covered seating areas at each of the hairpin turns, so anyone finding the ascent too difficult, can always sit down and take a breather before tackling the next ramp.

As Fred had suggested that the day's activities should begin with the beach petanque, they all used this path to descend to the promenade and from there, walked along it in the direction of the pier. When they saw what they considered to be a suitable spot for their game, Fred, Tom and John stepped across onto the beach and George continued on towards the pier. He wouldn't need to ring them to find out where they were, as the petanque game would take some time.

"No throwing the jack into the middle of a rock pool this time," said Tom. "I got my shirtsleeve wet trying to retrieve it last year and there was a crab in there which I swear was giving me a filthy look."

"All right," said John, "but accidents do happen and the rock pools do make the game more interesting."

Fred and Tom made up one team and played against John on his own, until George got back from the pier. John didn't mind this, as it meant that he could throw George's boules as well as his own, giving him some extra practice and more opportunity to get his eye in.

The game started and it wasn't long before a small crowd gathered on the promenade to watch them. The sight of three older gentlemen throwing multi-coloured balls up and down the beach seemed to have a certain fascination and their game soon had quite an appreciative audience.

"Good shot, sir," shouted one of their supporters, as Tom's boule landed right next to the jack.

"Who's winning?" yelled another.

"The red and blue team are in the lead at the moment," John answered, "but you just wait until my team's star player arrives."

At the pier ticket office, George was busy showing his printed booking confirmation to the woman he'd had problems with the previous day. His name was clearly displayed, as was the fact that he had used PayPal to pay for the transaction.

The woman studied it for a few minutes, before coming to her conclusion. "It shows both PayPal and George Wilson on this confirmation," she announced, "so I think it's possible that someone might have made a mistake when the booking was copied onto our system."

"Hardly rocket science," George muttered under his breath.

She fussed around for quite a few minutes more and then finally handed George four printed tickets. "I hope you and your friends enjoy tonight's show Mr Paypal," she said.

Back on the beach, the game was well advanced and Fred and Tom were still in the lead by a couple of shots. As George joined them, he was rather surprised when the small group of watchers on the promenade immediately began clapping and cheering him. He didn't know that they were greeting the arrival of what they thought was the star player.

When it came to his shot, George's boule missed the target altogether and rolled down the beach and into the surf. This was hardly what the spectators had expected to see from a star player and they quickly lost interest in the game and began wandering off.

"Is that the best you can do?" asked John. "I was doing better on my own."

They played a total of twenty ends and Fred and Tom managed to continue to hold on to their slight lead. They were declared the winners. The exertion of repeatedly having to throw the boules and all that walking up and down the beach had taken its toll and everyone was in agreement that the next item on the agenda should be to sit down somewhere with a nice cup of tea.

There is an outdoor café on the promenade, so they made their way there and sat at one of the tables. Tom went to get the teas and Fred began writing the results of the petanque competition on the score sheet he was carrying.

From out of his pocket, John produced a small blue metal box, which he opened to reveal two hexagonal chrome plated metal dice. This was his set of 'Owzthat' and contained all the equipment needed for a game of schoolboy cricket.

The idea of the game is just like any other cricket match. Teams of batsmen all try to score as many runs as possible before their last man is out. Our boys play the game with four teams of ten. The two dice each have six flat surfaces and are respectively called the 'batsman's' dice, which is marked: '1, 4, 3, 2, 6 and Owzthat' and the 'bowler's' dice, which is marked: 'bowled, caught, not out, stumped, LBW and no ball.'

The first team player rolls the batman's dice and as it must come to rest on a flat side because of its shape, there will always be a flat side uppermost as well. The figure on the top face indicates the number of runs made and is added to the batsman's score sheet. He then rolls again and continues to build up his run total, until the word 'Owzthat' comes up on the top face of the dice.

It is then the bowler's turn and he rolls the bowler's dice. If it comes to rest with 'not out' or 'no ball' uppermost, then the batsman continues his turn. Any other result means that the batsman is out and that team's second batsman then takes over. Play continues until all ten batsmen are out and the team's total score for the innings is recorded.

Play then passes to the second team and continues in the same way, until all four players have had an innings each. The team with the most runs wins.

The beauty of the game is that it can be played almost anywhere, as all that is required is a flat surface on which to roll the dice. If the weather is inclement, then the game can continue indoors, so there is no likelihood of rain ever stopping play in a game of Owzthat.

The table at the outdoor café on the promenade was not an ideal playing surface, as it was made of aluminium and rolling the metal dice on it made quite a clatter. Not that this concerned the boys all that much, but they did get a few dirty looks from people sitting at nearby tables.

Tom seemed to be on a winning streak, as he kept rolling sixes and whenever John had his turn to try and bowl him out, he kept coming up with 'no ball' or 'not out'. Tom's final score was 397 runs, which was a very respectable target for the other three to try and beat.

John only managed a miserable 127 runs, due in no small part to the fact that Fred proved to be a demon bowler and seldom failed to get John's batsmen out every time he rolled the bowler's dice.

Fred and George each scored 287 and 406 respectively, so George narrowly beat Tom and was declared the winner. He promptly suggested that they should all adjourn to the Old Boot for a congratulatory pint on him.

"It won't be open yet," Fred told him. "Let's go and check out the crazy golf course, to make sure that it looks good enough for our game tomorrow."

Crazy golf has always been the final competition in the boy's weekend since the very beginning. It has assumed an importance far greater than any of the other events and they all put everything they possibly can into trying to win this one.

George partners Tom every year, with John and Fred against them. This splits the golf players into different teams, not that this matters very much when playing crazy golf on the Cromer course. Any advantage a skilled putter may have counts for very little, as the playing surface at Cromer bears more resemblance to a moonscape, than to any perfectly manicured putting green.

The course is located on a patch of land just off the main road. It is right behind the boating lake, which is a one foot deep puddle of water where you can hire a canoe to paddle round an oval circle with a concrete island in the middle. A complete circuit only takes about two minutes - and that's for a very slow paddler. There is also a bungee trampoline on the site, which is restricted to children's use only.

Many crazy golf courses have angled concrete channels, through which you need to guide your ball towards the hole at the far end, negotiating some obstacle on the way. These obstacles can take the form of things like windmills with rotating sails, which you need to pass through without your ball getting knocked off course by the sail, and various other ingenious structures, all designed to make the course more complicated.

Cromer doesn't go in for anything like that. When it opens each morning, someone fetches the eighteen worn-out fibreglass 'obstacles' from the hut on site and positions them around the course. They come in all sorts of shapes and sizes (some of them even have ramps at the front) but the thing they all have in common is that there is a hole (or holes) at the front and a single hole out the back. Your ball needs to be hit though these obstacles and when it exits on the other side, always assuming that it doesn't get stuck in the middle, there is a small shallow depression somewhere nearby, into which you must putt your ball. The positioning of the obstacles varies from year to year (and sometimes from day to day) and there are no set tee-off positions. Players just decide where to start on each hole for themselves.

The grass itself is very scrub-like and there are bare patches all around. The odd rabbit hole here and there adds to the fun, as do all the pieces of litter and dog-ends everywhere. These are counted as further obstacles and the dog-ends are sometimes useful as tee position markers.

All in all, the course could do with some improving, but it makes an appropriately challenging final event for the boys and is the competition they all look forward to the most.

Having surveyed the course and seen that it was in exactly the same state as last year, the boys walked back over to the promenade and sat down on a bench to gaze out at the sea. It was a moment of quiet relaxation while they waited for the pub to open and they sat there for nearly half an hour, just soaking up the atmosphere.

As it was now very nearly lunchtime, John decided that he would return to the hotel to find out what the situation was with regard to his car. He had been resisting the temptation of ringing the hotel all morning, but couldn't stand the suspense any longer. He wanted to know if anyone had turned up yet with a new set of wheels and tyres for his car. "I'm going to nip back to the hotel," he told the others.

"Well, you go there and give us a call to let us know what's happening," Fred suggested. "I'll go and drop our betting slips off at the bookies and we can all meet up at the Old Boot. Don't forget we are scheduled to play the pitch and putt course this afternoon, so I suppose we will need to get our clubs out of the car as well."

"Are you going to change into your plus fours and harlequin socks for the match?" Tom asked. Fred had worn such an outfit the previous year, but had only done so to wind up John and George, who as the golfers of the group took the pitch and putt match a little bit too seriously.

"I don't think I will bother this year," Fred replied. "It is embarrassing enough that we bring our own clubs to play with, instead of using the same ones as everyone else. All the other players watching assume that we are seasoned pros, until you and I make a cock-up on the first hole."

"That's a shame," Tom responded. "You did cut quite a figure wearing those short trousers and garish socks last year, especially with that flat cap on your head."

At the hotel, John was delighted to find that his car had been restored to its previous condition and was no longer perched on bricks. There was now a shiny new wheel on each corner and the tyres were brand new as well. The fitter was just about to leave as he got back, so he spoke to the man before he left.

"I must say you've done a good job and remarkably quickly too," he told him. "I must commend you and your company on giving such outstanding service."

"We're used to it mate," the fitter replied. "Yours are the fifth set of wheels I've had to replace this month. I reckon there must be a gang of wheel thieves operating in the area."

"Maybe not for that much longer," John told him. "This lot managed to get caught on camera while they were in the act of stealing my wheels."

"Oh well," said the fitter, "just as I was beginning to get used to all that extra money at overtime rates."

7

THE GOLDEN CRAB

John looked pleased with himself when he met the others at the Old Boot. What could have turned the weekend into a disaster had been resolved with minimal difficulty. He knew he would have to pay the nominal excess on his insurance policy, but the claim would not affect his no-claims bonus, as that was protected. He had also managed to pick up a plateful of whelks for himself on the way back, without the others knowing that he had done so.

The rest were all talking excitedly when he arrived and he wondered what it was all about. "What's going on?" he asked.

"George has just come up with a brilliant idea," Fred told him and proceeded to explain, "Apart from the fact that we come here every year, what else is Cromer famous for?"

"Sun, sea, sand, beach, pier . . ." John started reeling off all the things he thought the answer might be.

"No," said Fred, "you're missing the really obvious one."

"I give up," John replied. "You will have to tell me."

"Cromer is famous for its crabs," the others all shouted at him simultaneously.

"So I thought," George told him, "that we could all have a go at crabbing."

"But none of us are anglers and we don't know the first thing about catching crabs."

"But that's the beauty of it," said George. "There is absolutely nothing to it. All you need is a bit of string with a weight on the end and some bait. You just dangle your line over the side of the pier and when a crab grabs your bait, you just pull it in."

"What on earth made you think of that?" John asked.

George explained that when he had been walking along the pier earlier that morning, he had noticed how many people were crabbing and suddenly realised that it was an activity they had not thought of including in their weekend.

"Some of them were catching quite big ones as well," George said, "and that includes some of the kids. If they can do it, then so can we. The crabs won't know that we're not experts." He produced a reel of fishing line from his pocket and four big shiny metal washers that he had just been and picked up from one of the hardware stores in town.

"What would we use for bait?" John asked.

"Right there on that table," Tom told him. John's

eyes followed the direction of Tom's outstretched arm to another table, where somebody had left a half eaten bacon, lettuce and tomato baguette. "Crabs love bacon," Tom knowledgably advised.

"Can we fit it into the schedule Fred?" John said.

"Providing we only spend an hour or so at it," Fred replied, "then we will need to get over to the pitch and putt course for our match."

They quickly finished their pints (John didn't have one) and Tom strolled over to the other table, where he grabbed hold of what remained of the baguette and walked off with it.

As they left the pub courtyard, a woman turned to her husband and said, "Did you see that? Those poor old buggers are spending all their money on beer and then can't afford to feed themselves. What is the world coming to when pensioners have to descend to the level of stealing scraps of food other people have left?"

At the pier, George gave everybody a length of line and a washer and they quickly assembled their fishing gear. The contents of the BLT were torn apart and everyone received some bacon to use as bait.

"Do you think it is worth adding a lettuce leaf as well?" John asked.

Five minutes later and four new fishing lines dangled over the side of the pier. When George felt a slight pull on his line, he quickly jerked back and began to pull it up. "I've caught one!" he shouted, but when his line surfaced, there was nothing but the shiny washer on the end.

"You're doing it all wrong!" said a little kid who was passing by. "You can't hook a crab, that's not the way it works. They grab hold of your bait with their claws and if you pull them in gently, they will still be holding onto it when you get them to the surface."

"Nothing to it is what you said," commented John, addressing George. "That young kid knows more about crabbing than you do."

George just muttered something about never having claimed to be an expert anyway and everyone returned to the task in hand.

John was the first one to actually catch a crab, but he took so long to gently pull it in that the crab had finished off the bacon by the time it reached the surface. They just had a momentary glimpse of it as it let go of the line and sank back down to the bottom.

Half an hour later and all they had to show for their efforts was just one small crab. It was no more than an inch and a half across and looked even smaller in the plastic kitchen bucket they had purchased to hold their catch.

"I told you we only needed a small bucket," said Fred. "That poor thing looks lost in there."

The tiny crab hadn't managed to eat much of the bacon on the line, so John decided to give it some more. He dropped a few pieces into the bucket. "It just needs feeding up a bit, that's all," he declared, "then it will grow into something more sizeable."

"Not by the time we leave tomorrow lunchtime," George pointed out.

Tom suddenly felt his line being tugged quite hard and began pulling it up. There wasn't a prize for winning, but it would be one in the eye for George if he could land the largest crab. George was the one who had narrowly beaten him at Owzthat.

The line certainly felt quite heavy and he concentrated on pulling it up slowly but steadily. He was going to get lucky and be the one who actually caught something worthwhile. There were gasps of surprise as the crab broke the surface, still happily hanging onto Tom's bacon bait. It was a good eight inches across, but what amazed them most was its appearance. The top of the crab's shell was bright gold in colour, which is not the colour crab shells are meant to be.

More by luck than anything to do with skill, Tom managed to lift the crab up to the level of the pier railings without it dropping off. George took hold of it with both hands, making sure that that he kept his fingers well clear of its huge menacing looking claws.

He held it up for everyone to see. "That's a real whopper," Fred exclaimed, as George waved it about in front of the other crabbers along the side of the pier.

"You've caught the golden crab!" one of them said excitedly, "You lucky sod!" The four friends looked at each other with confused expressions and

George placed the golden crab in the bucket. The little crab had been happily enjoying its bacon when the larger one suddenly dropped in, but it immediately forgot all about that as it frantically searched around for somewhere to hide (which is rather difficult at the bottom of a round bucket).

"What do you mean by the golden crab?" asked Tom.

What they didn't know was that Cromer Council had come up with the idea of painting the top of a crab's shell with gold paint, before dropping it back into the water by the pier. Crabs are quite fond of the area around the base of the pier, so they didn't think it would stray too far from there.

This had happened just after Easter (at the start of the tourist season) and marked the launch of a major competition, with a big prize for the lucky person who recaptured the golden crab. There was a huge publicity campaign at the time, but as the season wore on and the wily crustacean continued to successfully evade capture, most everyone had completely forgotten all about the gold coloured crab lurking somewhere beneath the pier.

It was now more than a month since any of the Cromer papers had even mentioned the competition and the local councillors had more or less given up hope of the damn thing ever being caught.

There had been a few jokers attempting to cheat, by painting a crab gold and trying to pass it off as the golden crab, but the council weren't completely stupid. Although it had not been publicised, they had placed a special mark on the underneath of the crab, so only a crab with this special marking could be the genuine one.

The boys knew nothing at all about any of this and listened with interest as one the other crabbers told them all about it. "I've been trying to catch that thing for months," he said, "then you jokers come along with a bit of string and some bacon and catch it in less than an hour."

"Well what do we do now?" Tom asked. "Who do we need to see to tell them that I've caught it?"

"I don't know," said the man, "but I suppose you could have a word with the pier manager. He is employed by the council after all."

Needless to say, the manager wasn't in his office as he didn't work on Saturdays. There was however an emergency phone number for contacting him.

Tom dialled the number and listened to a recorded message. He looked at the others and said, "This message is asking me to provide full details of the emergency and then someone will get back to me. What should I say?"

"I wouldn't have thought catching that crab counts as an emergency," Fred suggested, "but you could always say that there has been an incident on the pier and that you need some assistance."

Tom looked thoughtful for a moment as he tried to think of what to say and then dialled the number again. He spoke into the phone for a minute or so and then hung up. "Well, I've left him a message," he said. "I suppose all we can do now is to wait."

They felt like idiots, standing there with a bright red plastic bucket with two crabs in it, but there was little else they could do. Fred was beginning to worry about his schedule, as they were running late for the start of the pitch and putt competition.

When the police car and ambulance squealed to a halt at the entrance of the pier, the others began to wonder what message Tom had actually left for the pier manager. It had certainly stirred things up.

One of the policemen was the same sergeant they had seen at the hotel. "Not you lot again!" he said. "Do you know what's happened? We've been told that there's been a serious accident on the pier."

"I've caught the golden crab," Tom said, realising immediately that this wasn't perhaps the best thing to say in the circumstances. "We didn't know who to tell, so I rang the pier manager and left a message on his ansaphone."

"You've caught what?" queried the sergeant. "Is it contagious?"

It took a while to sort everything out, by which time the ambulance had left and the policemen were actually quite relieved. The last thing any of them needed on a quiet Saturday afternoon was a real emergency on the pier.

As it happened, the police sergeant turned out to be reasonably understanding about it all and agreed to telephone the leader of the council at his home. After talking on the phone for a while, he turned back to the boys and said, "There is nothing can be done before the council offices open on Monday morning. You will need to go there and take the golden crab with you."

"But we won't be here on Monday morning," John told him. "We are going home tomorrow."

The police sergeant explained this to the councillor on the phone and after listening for a couple more minutes, ended the conversation.

"Right," he said, "Here's what you need to do."

He explained that they would have to take photographs of the golden crab and that these must include one of its underneath. These they should then send to the council's publicity office and if it turned out that Tom's crab was the genuine one, then the council would contact him and tell him what was to happen next. "Congratulations, by the way," the police sergeant said.

The four of them looked down into the bucket, where the golden crab was still menacingly waving its huge claws about. Nobody fancied the idea of reaching down in there to pull the crab out for its photo shoot.

"So what do we do with the crab after we have taken its picture?" Tom asked.

"That's up to you," the sergeant replied. "You might like to get it stuffed and mounted as a souvenir of your visit to Cromer, or you could of course always eat it!"

8

PITCH AND PUTT

After the policeman had left, they suddenly realised that they hadn't asked him if he knew what the prize was.

"I daresay we will find out in due course," said Tom. "Now how on earth are we going to take some photographs of this beast?"

The problem was solved when the kid who had advised them on the correct way to go crabbing walked by again. "I hear you've caught the golden crab," he said. "What are you going to do with it?"

Fred explained that they needed to pull it out of the bucket to take some photos, but that none of them felt brave enough to put their hands in to pick it up.

"You are a right bunch of wimps for old geezers, aren't you?" the kid said scornfully, as he reached into the bucket and lifted out the crab.

The required pictures were taken on Tom's mobile phone, including the one from below. This revealed the letters 'CDC' painted on the bottom of the shell. "I bet that stands for Cromer District Council," remarked Fred.

When the kid put the crab down on the pier's plank decking after the photo session, it immediately scuttled off sideways and the last anyone saw of it was when it reached the edge of the pier and tumbled back into the sea. "Well, at least that solves the problem of what to do with it," George observed.

They thanked the kid for his help and Tom then e-mailed the pictures to the council. There was no problem finding the right address to send them, as it was displayed on one of the posters outside the pier manager's office.

"We need to get over to the pitch and putt course," Fred said. "We are really running late now and if we don't get a move on, there won't be time to fit everything in."

John had had the foresight to bring his car from the hotel, so it was now parked in the car park by the pitch and putt course.

"Well, at least that saves us having to waste even more time going back to the hotel for the clubs," Fred commented.

They walked over to the car park and collected the clubs from the Jaguar. George and John had brought along their golfing shoes, so they put these on. Fred and Tom were quite happy to play in the trainers they were wearing. Whatever they had on their feet wasn't going to influence how they played golf in the slightest, as they were both totally useless at it.

The chap in charge of the pitch and putt golf course was still the same one. He had been there every year since they first started coming to Cromer and he recognised them as soon as they walked up.

He was about fifty years of age and too young to remember much about the swinging sixties. This did not however stop him trying to look the part. He had long thinning grey hair, tied up in a ponytail at the back, and both his ears were pierced, with multiple rings hanging down from them. A straggly beard obscured his chin and he had a long droopy moustache, which was very heavily stained by the countless roll-ups he continuously smoked. None of the boys could remember ever seeing him without a dog-end hanging out from one corner of his mouth. His arms and legs (and possibly other parts of his anatomy as well) were completely covered in tattoos and he wore an old white cotton cloth shirt, blue jeans and plastic flip-flops on his feet.

As the boys approached his little shed, they could hear the strains of sixties music blaring out from whatever music playing device he kept inside. "Hi there guys," he called out. "Are you going to have a go at beating the course record this year?"

The course record had been set by a fifteen year old boy three years previously. John and George would love to beat it, but knew they had no hope at all with Tom and Fred as their partners.

There had been an occasion two years previously,

when Tom couldn't play because of an injury and Fred had suggested that he would drop out as well, to allow John and George to play a round of singles. Neither of them got within six strokes of the record and immediately claimed that the boy's score was totally impossible and that he must have lied about how many strokes it had taken him. They didn't like the fact that they had not been able to match the youngster's score.

"No," John answered. "It's just a friendly match today. I don't think any of us will be going for the record."

"Still brought your own clubs with you though, I see," sixties man commented. They paid for their round of golf and walked over to the first tee, which was no more than an area of worn out plastic grass, sitting on top of a slight mound. They were ready to start their game.

It was Fred to tee off first and it took him several attempts to get his ball to balance on the little plastic tee that he'd had to virtually hammer into the hard ground with the end of his club.

"Fore!" he shouted, before he'd even taken a swipe at his ball.

"You only say that when you've hit a ball and it goes off in the wrong direction," George told him.

"Well my ball certainly won't go where I want it to, so I thought I'd save a bit of time and warn people first."

The first hole on the pitch and putt course is a dogleg to the green (that is to say it is crooked like a dog's hind leg) and most players aim for the bend and then take their next shot from there. Anyone attempting to take the short cut to the green has to try and avoid the bunker that has been cunningly positioned immediately in front of it.

Fred's ball missed the bend, missed the bunker and shot off to roll onto the fairway for the fourth hole.

John stepped up next and took a few practice swings before driving straight at the green. His ball landed in the bunker.

"Texas scramble rules apply, remember," John told them. Fred and Tom just looked at each other, not knowing what the hell he was talking about. John and George were forever coming out with strange golfing terms that they didn't understand.

"You might need to explain that rule again," Tom suggested.

Texas scramble is a team event, where the players on each team decide which of their initial shots is in the best position. Both team members then take their second shot from that spot, irrespective of where the other team member's ball ended up. The game continues like this from hole to hole and by always using the most favourable ball position for the team's next shot, it theoretically means that the poorer players do not handicap the better ones.

George's ball ended up in the middle of the bend, and as his partner's ball had landed a considerable distance away (on the fourth fairway in fact) he decided that he and Fred should play from where his own ball was positioned.

Anywhere was better than the bunker into which John had driven his ball, so when it came to him and Tom deciding which ball position to play from, they chose the spot where Tom's ball was resting.

"What was it Mark Twain said about golf?" Tom asked Fred, as they trudged from hole to hole following the two enthusiasts.

"Something about it being the best way to spoil a good walk in the country, I think," Fred replied.

There is a particularly wicked hole on the course, as the green itself is positioned on a steep incline. Balls rarely come to rest on this slope, but run off down the hill to end up far away. A putt that misses the hole by just an inch may finally come to rest fifty yards away, so you either need to be very accurate (or very lucky) to achieve the par four suggested for the hole.

George and Fred were leading by one hole when the boys reached this one. "Try to land in the rough next to the green," George suggested to Fred. "That will give us our best chance when it comes to putting." George's own ball had disappointingly ended up so far away as to not be worth considering.

Fred tried to oblige, but his ball landed on the green and then raced off down the slope until it was almost out of sight.

"Just do what you think is best," John suggested to Tom.

Tom carefully sighted up on his ball and took a

swing. He missed the ball completely. "That was just a practice shot," he declared. "You are not counting that one, are you?"

Everyone agreed that as he hadn't actually hit his ball (even though he had intended to) his air shot would not count as a stroke.

Tom had another go and this time chipped it to land exactly where any professional would have wanted his ball to be. It was only two inches off the edge of the green and less than six feet from the pin.

"Jammy bugger," said Fred. "I suppose you're now going to tell us that you played for that?"

"I do have my moments of brilliance," Tom replied.

It was now George and Fred's team to play first, as Tom's ball was nearer the pin than either of theirs. George's ball wasn't where he wanted it, but was better placed than Fred's. Accordingly, Fred was sent off to retrieve his ball, as he would also need to play from where George took his shot. He tramped off down the hill and returned a few minutes later, completely out of puff.

George's chip shot went close to the hole, but not close enough. It paused momentarily, before it ran off down the hill to end up somewhere near where Fred's ball had been a few minutes earlier. When Fred played from the same position, his ball didn't even reach the hole before starting off down the slope again. Both their balls were now sitting fifty yards away and it was John and Tom's turn to play.

"Texas scramble rules remember," John said. "You pair will need to play from right down the bottom of the hill." He took his shot from where Tom's ball was positioned and did exactly the same thing as George. There were now three balls down the bottom of the hill and only Tom left to play.

Everyone expected Tom's ball to join the others but by the merest fluke, he achieved a miracle shot. His ball actually missed the hole by a good four inches and travelled a foot past it before stopping. It then hung there for just a moment, before slowly starting to roll down the slope. By the luckiest of chances, the hole was directly in its line of travel, so his ball dropped straight in. The cheers from John and Tom could probably be heard as far away as Sherringham and even sixties man in his hut stopped to look over in their direction.

George threw his club to the ground in disgust and Fred just creased up laughing. John and Tom were leaping up and down and hugging each other. It was only a single hole, but the scores were now level and there were only six holes left to play.

"Do you realise," John was telling Tom, "that you only took two shots on that hole and that it is a par four? You have just got an eagle, which is something you don't see that many players do."

The game didn't go well for George and Fred after this hole and when Fred missed his putt on the sixteenth, John cried out, "We win three and two!"

He had reverted to using one of those weird golfing terms that Fred and Tom didn't understand.

"But we haven't finished yet," said Fred. "There are still two more holes to play."

John patiently explained that winning three and two meant that as he and Tom were leading by three holes, with only two holes left to play (three and two) that George and Fred couldn't possibly win, whatever happened on the last two holes. The match was therefore already over and there was no point in continuing to play.

"I think there is," said Tom. "We've paid to play the full eighteen holes, so we should at least have a go at all of them, just to get our money's worth."

"Well, I'm not going to stand here listening to you pair gloating," George said stroppily. "I'm going over to the community club for a beer and will see you there when you've finished messing about."

As George walked away, Tom turned to Fred and said, "Isn't it always the way with all these golfing enthusiasts? The moment things don't go their way, they start getting all upset."

They decided that it wasn't worth continuing the game with just the three of them, so they took the clubs back to the car and then joined George in the community club.

9

CROMER'S ATTRACTIONS

Cromer Community Club is a very popular place and has a large membership. It also opens its doors to the many tourists who visit Cromer (providing they are signed in) and has a large well stocked bar, which offers food as well. There are more than enough chairs and tables to go round and it is a comfortable place to have a quiet pint and a game of pool, dominoes, darts or cards. Most weekends there is an evening show of some sort and the boys regularly wished that they had a place like this nearer to where they lived.

When John, Tom and Fred walked in, George was already practicing on the pool table. Their pool matches used to be played in the Hotel Splendide, which is a large and imposing building, dating back to the Victorian era. It sits in a commanding cliff top position in the centre of town and at the head of the pier, with views over the beach and out to sea. There is very limited parking at the front of the hotel and none whatsoever anywhere else.

Many of the streets in the centre of Cromer are quite narrow and there is a particularly narrow one at the rear of the hotel. This means that any coaches bringing guests to the Hotel Splendide completely block the street and cause traffic jams all around the town. This probably wouldn't be that much of a problem if the guests and their luggage could be transferred into the hotel fairly quickly, but this never happens for one very good reason.

It would be fair to say that the Hotel Splendide mostly caters for the older generation, but many of them look like they've just escaped from a geriatric ward. Every time a coach delivers a new batch of these frail and elderly guests, there is always a long delay while the driver unloads all the zimmer frames and other walking aids first. He then has to help everyone down the steep steps from the coach, while trying to ensure that they have not forgotten to bring their walking sticks, portable bottles of oxygen and colostomy bags with them.

Having got them all off the coach, the driver is then faced with the problem of trying to round up the ones who have strayed away from the group. Most of these probably lost their minds years ago and having arrived somewhere new, have wandered off in the vague hope of finding them again.

After everyone has been found, he then needs to try to shepherd them into the hotel through the rear entrance, providing he can get them past the doorway without half of them stopping to admire their surroundings and creating a bottle neck. It could be worse though, as the front entrance to the hotel has a set of revolving doors and the prospect of attempting to get fifty or so doddery old codgers through them doesn't even bear thinking about.

Most of the drivers also have to make several return trips to the coach, because a number of the ancients will invariably have left something on their seats.

The entire process can take up to an hour, by which time all traffic in the town has ground to a standstill. The harassed driver then returns to his coach and drives off, allowing normality to return to the town centre for a brief period, before another coachload of elderly guests arrives and the same thing happens all over again.

It was not the company of all the veteran holidaymakers which prompted the boys to select the Hotel Splendide as the venue for their pool matches. It was the fact that it had a huge games room, with a darts board, a ping-pong table and a full size pool table, which was in excellent condition as few of the hotel guests ever used it. It was also nice and quiet in the evening, because most of the residents went to bed very early. The bar was near the games room, so they could take their drinks in there and have a relaxed game of pool. There was even a table that they occasionally used to play their Owzthat match.

It was of course too good to last and when they turned up to play pool two years previously, they discovered that the games room had been converted into extra bedrooms. There was nothing else for it but to find another venue, which posed a few problems, as most of the tables in all the other pubs and hotels in Cromer are in such poor condition as to make them virtually unplayable.

The problem was solved when sixties man at the pitch and putt course mentioned to them about the community club. They had seen the place before but had never actually been in it. He told them that the club welcomed visitors and when they actually asked whether they could play pool there, the staff were more than willing to let them do so. They had played their annual pool matches at the community club ever since.

The table in the club is immaculately maintained and there is quite a wide choice of cues as well (most of which have still got tips on them). There can be no blaming the table or your cue when shots go wrong, if you are playing pool in Cromer Community Club.

For the individual pool matches, all four of the boys needed to play one game each against all the others, which meant playing six games. For the doubles matches, they usually played five games, unless one team was in an unbeatable position after three or four had been played.

Tom was to partner George in the team event, against Fred and John. They decided to play the doubles first, so George and Tom immediately went into a huddle to discuss tactics. Fred and John just watched in amusement, as they were both quite good players and felt reasonably sure that they would win. Whereas the others all had pints, John only had a half pint, because he was on driving duty.

Their confidence was rewarded, as they won the first two games easily. George and Tom won the next one, meaning that if Fred and John could win just one more game, then they would be the champions. The fourth game was very closely fought, but ended when Tom accidently potted the black ball. John and Fred had won and the entire match had only taken a little more than an hour.

It was now four thirty in the afternoon and there wasn't enough time to play the singles matches, as they wanted to take a stroll around the shops before they shut. The show didn't actually start until eight in the evening, but they always went to the Old Boot for a pint first and would need to be in the theatre by seven forty five at the latest, if they intended to place an order for drinks during the interval (which they always did).

There are a lot of shops in Cromer, many of which sell gifts and souvenirs. There is also a place where you can buy retro-sweets, while another specialises in selling handmade chocolates. Finding a bucket and spade for the beach is never going to be a problem and an old book shop and several antique emporiums cater for those with more discerning tastes. There is something for everyone, so a tour of Cromer's shops is always interesting.

One of the boys' favourite places to visit is the local butcher's shop in the High Street. The proprietor can still regularly be found behind the counter and the shop has been there since 1985. It is very difficult to miss his shop, because there is a life-sized smiling plastic butcher standing by the entrance. The quality of the meat sold there is very high and the boys never come to Cromer without calling in make a few purchases.

Fortunately, the hotel where they stay is prepared to store whatever they buy in the fridge overnight, so as long as they remember to ask for everything back before they leave, the system works quite well. They could of course bring a cold box with them and purchase a bag of ice to go inside it, but they have been trying to remember to do that for five years now and yet still always have to rely on the hotel fridge.

Tom bought four huge sausage pinwheels and Fred opted for a good supply of different handmade sausages. George went for the pork chops and John couldn't resist a huge lamb shank, which was twice the size of the ones on offer at his local butchers and priced very reasonably. They struggled out through the door with two big carrier bags bulging with succulent delights.

"I suppose I should buy the wife some chocolates to keep her happy," John said, as they were passing the shop. He went in, leaving to others to continue wandering around the other stores. At least he had got out of having to carry one the carrier bags.

Tom went into one of the shops where they sold all sorts of different coloured sticks of rock and other confectionary souvenirs of the seaside. He bypassed the ones with 'Cromer' running through the middle of them and went straight to the rack where they kept the novelty ones. After a few minutes struggling to read what some of them said, he finally found one which he thought was perfect and purchased it.

Outside the shop, he showed it to Fred and George. "I bought it for the missus," he said. "She's going to hate me for it." The others held it endwise so that they could read what it said inside. The message running through the middle of the stick of rock was: 'Suck on this!'

Some of the shops were now beginning to close so they decided to call in at the Queen's Arms, where they knew they would be able to watch the football results and find out whether anybody had correctly predicted the results of the six matches they had all picked. They had lost John by now, so called him on his mobile to let him know where they would be.

The barmaid at the pub turned the television on for them, but was new and had no idea how to work it. "You will just have to play with it until you find what you're looking for," she said, handing them three different controllers to try. The secret of operating this particular television set relied on selecting the correct network with one of these controllers and then using one of the others to find the correct channel. The problem was that they all looked very similar and they didn't know which one was which. It took a great deal of fiddling before they finally managed to tune into the BBC's 'Final Score' program, by which time, John had arrived and accepted the half pint of beer they bought him. They then began examining each other's selections.

"If you get all six correct," Tom told George, "you will win £798.34. I will only win £14.23."

"But that's because you bet on all the favourites," George told him. "You can't expect to win much if you do that."

Fred's potential winnings amounted to £406.80 and John, who had made his predictions on the basis of creating a pretty pattern on his betting slip, would win £187.63.

"Did I just hear that Liverpool won?" John asked. "That's one of the teams I picked. Can't you turn the volume up on that thing?"

George slid the three controllers across the table to him. "You try," he said, "but don't lose the bloody program."

John decided not to risk it and they all strained their ears to hear the various final scores they were waiting for.

Out of his odds-on favourites, Tom had picked five correctly. George had four and Fred, as the other football supporter, had only managed to score three. John's pretty pattern actually produced five correct results, so he and Tom both had the same number. John was however declared the winner, as the six matches he had selected had longer odds than the ones chosen by Tom. He accordingly won the £4.00 pot. Nobody won any money from the bookies, but then they had only wagered a pound each to begin with.

"The next round is on John," announced Fred. "I hope you enjoy spending your ill-gotten gains." John immediately got up and bought three more beers. He didn't get one for himself, as he still needed to drive the car back to the hotel.

It was nearly six by the time they finished the last of their beers and time to go back and get ready for the evening show at the end of the pier.

The other three walked back while John went to get the Jaguar. It wasn't worth driving to the pub to pick them up, as there was always the possibility that a coach might be delivering another batch of elderly guests to the Hotel Splendide and he didn't want to risk getting trapped in town because of the traffic jam this always caused.

They all reached the hotel at about the same time and agreed to meet outside at six forty five. The End of the Pier Show was always enjoyable and they were all looking forward to it very much.

10

THE END OF THE PIER SHOW

The dress code for the End of the Pier Show is not at all formal, as most of the audience are on holiday and are unlikely to have brought suits and evening gowns with them. Anyone who does dress up in their finery will probably find themselves looking a bit out of place anyway. The boys wore shirts and slacks and carried fleeces with them, in case it turned a bit cool later on.

After their customary pint at the Old Boot, they walked to the entrance of the pier and joined all the other people making their way along it to the show.

The theatre itself is not actually right at the end of the pier. That place is taken by the lifeboat station, which has a slipway for launching Cromer's brand new lifeboat into the sea whenever there are any maritime emergencies to deal with. There is also a shop there, where people can support the R.N.L.I. by purchasing any of the various items on offer.

The Pavilion Theatre on the pier seats about five

hundred people and has a bar at front of house. It is a comfortable place to spend a few hours watching a show and the standard of the productions it stages is always very high. The performers themselves are all experienced professionals and the costumes, lighting and music are as good as one would expect to find in a West End theatre.

The End of the Pier Show is a good fun night out and features extracts from London musicals, variety and novelty acts and the obligatory comic or two. There is always a leading male and female singer and a dancing troupe and the entire ensemble takes part in the big set pieces, as well as all the individual performers taking their own turn on stage. Children from Marlene's School of Dance in Cromer always take part in the show and clearly enjoy doing so, from the happy expressions on all their little faces.

The golden rule for attending any show where a comic is likely to be on stage is never to sit in the first three or four rows. That is where you are most likely to get picked on, so the boys always book the middle of the fifth row. It is close enough to the stage to afford a really good view, but far enough back to generally escape the comic's attention.

The problem though is if you need answer the call of nature in the middle of a performance, as you then have to scramble past eight or so seated people in order to reach the end of the row. Tom always makes sure that he is well-watered before taking his seat. The very last thing he'd want to do is to draw attention to himself by having to get up for a wee in the middle of the show. That is even worse than sitting in the first few rows, as the comedians on stage always look out for it and the person doing so immediately becomes a target for their attention.

On this particular Saturday evening, the others had already taken their places while Tom was still in the toilet and had all sat down next to each other. This meant that he would have to sit at the end of their group, as opposed to somewhere in the middle. It was very easy for him to see which seat was his, as it was the only one left vacant in the entire row. He had to clamber past people to reach it, apologising to each of them in turn for the disruption.

When he finally reached his seat and sat down, he turned to George who was sitting next to him and said, "Thanks for waiting! I felt like a complete prat having to fight my way along the row all on my own."

He then glanced the other way, to see who was sitting on the other side of him. His mouth dropped open as he recognised the pretty young lady from the bookies. She gave him what could best be described as an icy glare and turned away.

The lights slowly dimmed and the music began. The show was about to start. As the curtains opened and the spotlights came on, the performers on stage launched into rousing version of one of the songs from 'Oklahoma'. The lead male singer was wearing a cowboy hat, checked shirt and jeans and belted out the number, while the girls in the dancing troupe (all wearing short gingham dresses and multi-layered frilly petticoats) were high-kicking their way round the stage.

There was so much gusset to be seen that an old man in the front row thought that he had died and gone to heaven. This was also one of the reasons why the boys liked to be near the front, as the girls were all very pretty and they each had their own personal favourite. There were also a couple of male dancers in the troupe, but only very few men in the audience ever paid that much attention to them.

At the end of the song, a backdrop came down and the comedian compère walked out on stage. "Good evening everyone," he said, "That was really something to see, wasn't it? . . . and that's just for starters!"

He walked to the front of the stage and over to one side, where he addressed a man in the second row. "Enjoying the show so far, sir?" he asked. "Is that your wife sitting next to you?"

The man stammered slightly as he replied, "It's my second wife actually."

The comic then looked at the woman for a moment before saying, "I don't blame you. She wouldn't have been my first choice either!"

The audience collapsed with laughter and the man turned red. His second wife was clearly not amused and he had to restrain her, to stop her storming the stage and attacking the comic.

The comedian ignored this and walked back across to the middle of the stage. It wasn't the first time he'd told that joke and it always helped to get the audience warmed up, even if it didn't go down too well with the couple he picked on.

"I've got some hot off the press news for everyone tonight," he continued. "Someone caught Cromer's golden crab today. I don't suppose that person is in the audience tonight, is he?"

Tom tried to make himself look invisible, as George kept nudging him in the ribs.

"Well," said the compère, "whoever caught it is a lucky fellow, as the council has offered a big prize to the competition winner."

The four boys all sat forward, eager to hear what Tom had won.

"What's the prize then?" someone from a few rows behind them shouted out.

"I'm glad you asked," the man on stage said. "I don't have all the details, but I know that part of the prize is a night on the town with this year's Miss Cromer."

There were "oohs!" and "aahs!" from all the audience and they broke into a spontaneous round of applause.

"What's more," he said, "I believe we have Miss Cromer here with us tonight. Would you please stand up and show us where you are, Miss Cromer."

The girl next to Tom slowly stood up and began

waving to different parts of the theatre. Tom wished that the earth would swallow him up.

"I'm sure our winner is here as well," the compère kept insisting, "Come on, don't be shy. Make yourself known, Mr Golden Crab Catcher."

Tom half raised an arm, but then thought better of it. He dropped it back on his lap, but not before Miss Cromer, who was just sitting down again, noticed.

"You're not the one who caught the golden crab, are you?" she screamed at him very accusingly. Tom meekly acknowledged by nodding his head and wished that he was somewhere else.

"Here's your winner," she shouted out in the direction of the stage. "He's a lecherous old man who likes to try it on with young ladies!"

For once in his life, the comedian on stage was struck dumb. He was frantically trying to think of something to say to defuse this volatile situation, when Fred yelled out, "He's not all that old!"

The audience burst out laughing again and the moment had passed. "All part of the show folks," the compère hastily announced. "Let's have a big hand for the gent. He's been a really good sport."

Everybody clapped and cheered for Tom, as Miss Cromer made her way to the end of the row and gave a final wave to the crowd, before disappearing out of the theatre.

"You're famous now Tom," said George. "How does it feel?"

The incident totally confused the audience. Half

of them thought it was all a joke and that it had been part of the act. Quite a few of the rest were staring in Tom's direction and wondering whether he really was a serial rapist.

The show continued with a juggler, who amazed everyone by precariously juggling various different shaped sharp objects in the air simultaneously. There was almost complete silence during his act, as everyone held their breath. The people in the front row were terrified that something might suddenly fly in their direction.

More song and dance routines followed and it didn't seem to be any time at all before the curtain was lowered again for the interval. The boys made their way to the Pavilion Bar and Tom sank his pint in one go. As pretty much everyone had pre-ordered their interval drinks, there wasn't much of a queue at the bar, so he was able to obtain a replacement fairly quickly.

They all went outside with their drinks and stood by the railings looking out to sea.

"It's been bloody good so far," said John, "and my little girl dancer is still looking as pretty as ever."

"So are you going to tell us all about you and Miss Cromer?" George asked. "I thought you were going to have a heart attack and die on the spot there for a moment. So where do you know her from? She's not some local girl you tried to chat up, is she?"

"I don't want to talk about it," Tom replied, as he

slurped another great mouthful of beer down his throat. "Let's just say that we've met."

"You need to slow down a bit Tom," John warned. "You know that beer goes straight through you."

The second half started with another big show song and then the girl dancers came on to perform a ballet. It was spellbinding and even though the boys knew nothing at all about ballet, they were just as engrossed as everyone else during this quiet and tasteful interlude. There were a few sniggers when the boy dancers joined in, as both of them were particularly well-endowed. The skin-tight tights they were wearing made this rather apparent.

The female comedienne had the boys creased up when she related the tale of baby balloon, which had got frightened during the night and went to join mummy and daddy balloon in their bed. Finding that there wasn't enough room for him to squeeze in, he let some air out of daddy balloon (she made a farting noise to simulate the sound of air escaping from a balloon). There still wasn't enough room in the bed, so baby balloon released some air out of mummy balloon (more sound effects). There still wasn't enough room for baby balloon, so he then let some air out of himself (even more appropriate farting noises). Finally, there was enough space for him to squeeze into the bed, so he got in and went to sleep.

By now, the audience were wondering where this story was going and some of them had tears in their eyes, from laughing so much at her enthusiastic rendering of farting sounds. When things settled down a bit, she carried on telling her tale.

When baby balloon went down to breakfast the following morning, mummy balloon told him that she knew what he had done during the night. "You've let me down and I'm very angry," mummy balloon said. "Your father feels that you've let him down as well."

The audience were cracking up by the time she delivered the punch line. "We're very disappointed with you and you should feel really ashamed. We both feel very let down and to make matters even worse . . . you let yourself down as well!"

The audience were creased up as the comedienne took her bow. The big finale came far too soon and as the boys left the theatre, some of the performers were in the Pavilion Bar, signing autographs and in the case of the singers, selling CD's that they had recorded.

They worked their way out through the throng and went out into the cooler night air. It was now about half past ten and they knew there would only be two sorts of places left open where they could sit down to eat an evening meal. Their choice was the Indian restaurant, or maybe a Chinese one.

They discussed these options as they strolled back down the pier towards the town.

11

THE HEIST

The food in the Chinese restaurant which the boys originally went to in Cromer was very good and they were well looked after. It was the first time that George had ever eaten Chinese (as he didn't hold with all that foreign muck) so they had to order for him, based on what they thought he might like. He found that he actually quite enjoyed the dishes he had and although this experience did not convince him to start ordering a Chinese takeaway on a regular basis, he was not against going back to this place again.

They went to the Indian restaurant the following year, but re-visited the Chinese the year after. Their expectations were dashed when the one waitress who was serving spent all her time talking to some young friends seated at another table. It was almost too much trouble to serve them and when she finally did, she got their order wrong and brought them a dish they hadn't asked for and failed to bring two of the dishes that they had ordered.

They then had the choice of either watching their food get cold or make a start on what they had, while the indifferent waitress returned to the kitchen to sort out her mistake. By the time their other two dishes finally arrived, they had eaten most of the rest, minus what they had wanted to go with them in the first place.

It spoiled an enjoyable day and they had not been back there since. There were other Chinese eating places, but they hadn't got around to trying them.

They had no complaints at all about the service at the Indian restaurant, although they still had the task of trying to order something that George might like. The only problem came when the restaurant changed hands. Dishes that had previously been medium curries suddenly became hot ones and the hot ones became so fiery as to make their eyes water and leave them gasping for air. They needed to adapt to how the new cooks cooked the dishes, but by now they knew what they were likely to get, so the Indian had become their restaurant of choice.

On their way to the Indian restaurant, they had to pass a jewellery shop and John noticed what he thought were flickering lights coming from the back of the store. They all pressed their faces against the shop window to peer inside. Their four squashed noses viewed from the other side would have made a wonderful photograph, had anyone been around to take one, but there was no one there to do so. They couldn't see anyone in the shop itself, but it looked like there were signs of activity in the back room.

Tom walked over to the entrance and gave the door an experimental push. He was very surprised when it opened and beckoned the others over. They all crept into the shop. The accumulative effect of all the pints of beer they had consumed during the day was giving them Dutch courage and they were feeling quite brave at that moment.

"Is there anybody there?" Tom called out. John (who was the most sober of all of them) walked over to a wall and tried to find the light switch. There was now no doubt at all that lights were moving about in the store room and a few moments later, a figure appeared in the doorway and shone a torch directly into their faces.

Tom, George and Fred all stood there looking like petrified rabbits caught in a car's headlights, but John was standing outside the beam of the torch. He found the light switch and flicked it on, instantly illuminating the entire shop.

The man in the doorway was wearing a balaclava over his head and was shocked when the lights came on. He was carrying a hammer, which he waved menacingly in the direction of the three (not quite so brave now) men standing in the middle of the shop. When he saw John, he wasn't quite sure who to wave his hammer at, so he kept switching from pointing it at John and trying to keep the other three covered.

Another man in a balaclava appeared behind him

and this one was clutching what looked like a tyre iron. They both stepped out from the store room and into the shop itself. "Clear off!" the first one shouted at the boys, "or you'll get what's for!"

John slowly walked over to join the others and then turned to look at the robbers. It was four against two, but the four were in their sixties and there was no telling the age of the two, because their faces were hidden. What could be seen however was that they both carried implements they could use as weapons, whereas the four were totally defenceless.

"I told you lot to bugger off," the man with the hammer said, now waving it at all four of them.

John took a step forward and stared straight into the man's eyes. "You obviously don't know this but I served in the SAS for ten years and could kill you with my bare hands, even if that hammer you are holding was a gun."

The robber looked down at the hammer in his hand and wished it was a gun. They fired bullets and worked at a distance. He would need to get closer to use his hammer.

"He's just bluffing," the second man said. "Knock his bloody head off!"

The first one wasn't so sure. John's gaze was totally unwavering. He looked as if he meant what he'd just said. The man looked at his companion in confusion.

"I can see you're not sure whether to believe me or not," said John coldly, "but just think about it.

Would I really face two armed men so calmly, if I wasn't sure that the pair of you didn't stand a chance? I really was a major in the SAS and will kill you both if you don't drop those weapons."

The man with the hammer took a step sideways so that the other robber was now directly in front of John. He didn't look quite so confident when he became the focus of John's steely glare.

"It's your choice," said John nonchalantly. "If I'm bluffing, then you will probably kill me. If I'm not, which I'm not, then you will be the ones who may die tonight."

The man with the iron bar took a step backwards. There was something about the way John just stood there that unnerved him.

"The question you need to ask yourself, punk," John almost spat out the words. "Do I feel lucky? . . . . . . Well, do you, punk?"

The hammer clattered to the floor, but the robber with the iron bar was still thinking about it. He was sure he'd heard the same words before, but couldn't quite remember where or when. At that moment, two police cars screamed to a halt outside the shop, with blaring sirens and flashing lights. The second robber dropped his iron bar immediately.

When the police dashed into the shop, they were astounded to see two men wearing balaclavas with their hands up and four older gentlemen just standing there. One of the policemen was the same sergeant the boys had already seen twice before.

"Not you lot again!" he said as he recognised

94

them. "What have you been up to this time? And who are these clowns in balaclavas?"

They explained how they had caught the thieves in the act of robbing the shop and as the police didn't seem to be around at the time, they had detained them while they waited for the police to arrive.

The two robbers were rapidly handcuffed and their balaclavas removed. The boys could see that they were barely out of their teens and did not look anything like as intimidating without their masks.

As they were being escorted out to the waiting police cars, the one who'd had the iron bar just had to ask, "Were you really in the SAS?"

John just smiled at him and said, "You'll never know son."

The police sergeant then returned to the shop. "They tripped the silent alarm when they broke in," he told the boys, "but it took me a while to round up enough officers to storm the place. I will need to get a statement from you four."

"Could you possibly do that while we are eating?" Fred asked. "If we don't get over to the Indian restaurant soon, it will be too late for us to get served.

The waiters in the restaurant were very surprised to see four rather late diners in the company of a policeman, but the sergeant quickly explained that they were heroes and deserved the very best treatment. They were shown to a table and Tom immediately ordered four large bottles of Cobra beer, before even looking at the menu. Another waiter stood by while they decided what to eat.

They each gave a statement to the police sergeant, but as they were all listening as each one did so, the four accounts were more or less identical. As he put away his notebook, the sergeant turned to them and said, "You four certainly know how to make the most of a weekend, don't you? If you are ever planning another one, perhaps you would you give me a call. I'd love to come along as well."

After the policeman had left, Fred turned to John and commented on the fact that it was news to him that he had ever been in the SAS.

"I never have been," John replied. "The nearest I ever got to the military was joining the CCF cadets when I was at school. My many years in senior management taught me how to take control of a situation when necessary and I often used to have to put people in their places. I just applied the lessons I learnt and tried to keep cool and sound convincing."

"You sounded just like Clint Eastwood's Dirty Harry there for a moment," Tom said, already half way through his Cobra. "I loved it when you asked that thug if he felt lucky and then called him a punk!"

"I was shitting bricks at the time," John told him. "I was terrified that he was going to call my bluff."

"But just supposing he had," George asked. "What on earth would you have done then? He might have killed you!"

"I don't think so," John said. "One of the other things I joined at school was the running club. I was the two hundred yards champion for three years running and still keep myself reasonably fit. I would have been out of that shop so fast that I would have made Usain Bolt appear slow."

They all laughed about it, but John had taken one hell of a chance and the outcome might have been completely different. Tom had finished his beer and was now signalling the waiter to get him another.

"You want to take it easy Tom," George warned him. "You have really been knocking them back today and you need to think about your prostate."

"I'm all right," said Tom, slurring slightly. "The meal will dilute the effects of the beer and you have to admit, it has been one hell of a day."

"So, come on Tom," urged John. "Tell us about you and Miss Cromer."

"I'm not that drunk yet." Tom responded. "Look. Here comes the food."

Some of the day's activities had worn them down a bit and they had squeezed an awful lot into a relatively short period. By now they all had quite an appetite so when their food arrived, they began to tuck into it with enthusiasm.

The day had started with the theft of John's wheels and had ended up with the attempted robbery at the jewellers. It had been the most excitement they had ever managed to fit into a single Saturday and set an impossible standard to try and repeat in future years. Tomorrow would be the crazy golf match and the jazz session on the way home. They probably wouldn't be able to fit in the singles pool matches, but these could always be played out at the Nag's Head. Fred didn't like it that his organised plan would need to be changed, but as the others kept telling him, schedules are not meant to be that rigid and he should learn to be flexible.

By the time they left the restaurant, they were all in high spirits. After a good night's sleep, they would be ready for whatever tomorrow might bring. Roll on Sunday.

12

TO PEE OR NOT TO PEE.
THAT IS THE QUESTION

The walk back from town to the hotel is up a slight hill. It is not that steep, but can be a bit taxing after a day spent expending energy. By the time they were half way back, Tom knew that he should have gone to the toilet again before he left the restaurant.

"I really need a wee," he told the others. "I don't think I can hold on long enough to get back to the hotel in time."

"You've got very little choice, chum," said Fred. "It's not that far, so you will just have to hang on until we get there."

"You don't know what it is like," Tom told him. "I feel like I'm going to pee in my pants and these are the only trousers I've brought with me."

"Try and put it out of your mind," John suggested. "You should think about something else. Imagine yourself lying on a beach somewhere, with just the sound of the children playing in the water and the surf gently surging up and down against the beach."

"That's the last thing I need to think about," Tom replied, as he gripped his thighs together even more tightly.

"Well, you could always think back to that trip you made to Niagara Falls," George said. "I remember you telling me how wonderful you thought it was to see so much water cascading down and splashing against the rocks below."

"Friends like you I need like a hole in the head," said Tom grimacing, as the pressure continued to mount.

They carried on up the hill, but had to keep stopping repeatedly. Tom's progress was painfully slow, because of the awkward way in which he had to walk.

"We are nearly at the hotel now," Fred pointed out. "One final burst of speed and we will be there."

"Don't talk about bursting," Tom told him. "I'm on the edge of doing that right now. I really don't think I can make it as far as the hotel."

Somehow Tom did manage to get there without having an accident, but then needed to sit down on the wall outside for a moment's rest. The thought of all those flights of stairs up to the toilet next to his room on the top floor didn't bear thinking about. He knew there was no way he would be able to climb them in the state he was in.

"It's just no good," he told the others. "I can't possibly hold on for a moment longer. He quickly looked around. There was not a soul in sight, other than the four of them. "I'm not going to do it right here in the main street though," he said. "I will go round the corner to the hotel entrance, where I will be out of sight of anyone passing by. You lot had better tag along and keep a lookout for me, just in case anyone does happen to come this way."

The others followed Tom round the corner and watched with some amusement, as he struggled to undo his fly. He flopped out his member, which by now was throbbing in expectation of doing one of the two things it had been specifically designed for.

The relief Tom felt, as all the pints of beer in his system vied for position with each other to exit his body first, could only be described as joy sublime. The pain he had been feeling gradually subsided, as his urine gushed out and splashed into the gutter, there to happily gurgle away down the drain.

"Ah!" he said, in a very long drawn out way. "That's better!" He glanced over his shoulder, expecting to see the other three standing there.

They had been quite prepared to stand and shelter him from view until the elderly couple suddenly appeared. The man and his wife had been out for a very late evening constitutional and were returning to the same hotel as the one the boys were staying at. John, Fred and George all made a run for it and dashed into the hotel, leaving Tom left standing there all on his own.

Tom had thought that as the hotel entrance was on a side road and out of sight around a corner, it would be safe for him to have a wee there. There was so little chance of anyone else seeing him. He hadn't banked on the elderly couple, who must have put on a quite a burst of speed to suddenly appear out of nowhere the way they had.

"Absolutely disgusting!" said the woman.

"I've got a prostate problem," Tom tried to explain. It might have been better if he could have controlled the flow and actually stopped peeing, but there was no possibility of that happening. Now that he had started he couldn't stop. His body had taken over and appeared to be determined to empty his bladder in one go.

"A man your age should set an example to the younger generation," the husband berated him, "and not behave like a lager lout!"

They passed him by and walked up the steps and into the hotel. Tom was more embarrassed than he had ever felt before in his life, as his offending member continued to pulsate with the surge of urine passing through it. By the time it had almost finished, he was virtually in tears. After a few final drips, the flow ceased and Tom was able to replace the now limp organ back in his pants. He zipped up his trousers.

He thought about how the others had left him all alone in this, his personal moment of anguish.

"You bastards!" he said with feeling.

He sat down on the wall again and lit a cigarette.

After a few minutes, John came out of the hotel and joined him. He had come out for a last cigar before going to bed.

"Why did you lot scarper and leave me there on my own?" Tom asked.

"Because we saw that old couple coming this way," John said, "and didn't want to be seen watching you pissing in the gutter. It would only have made things worse if we'd been caught as well."

"Thanks a million," said Tom. "I wouldn't have dreamt of deserting a friend at his moment of need!"

"Did they actually see what you were doing then?" John enquired, trying hard not to smile as he said it.

"Oh yes, they saw what I was doing all right," Tom replied. "In fact, they stopped and we all had a nice little chat about it."

"That's all right then. Are you feeling better now?"

"Good night John," Tom said, as he got up off the wall and went into the hotel.

On the way up to his room, Tom passed the twin room being shared by Fred and George. He could hear them laughing, even through the closed door, and knew exactly what they were laughing about. He hammered on the door and shouted out loudly, "You bastards!" The laughter inside the room suddenly stopped.

Tom turned away from their door and found

himself facing the elderly couple he'd seen outside. They were on the way back to their room from the bathroom down the hall. The old man frequently accompanied his wife to the toilet, as she sometimes had trouble getting up off the seat on her own and needed his assistance.

"I'm so very sorry about that," Tom spluttered profusely. "I can't imagine what you pair must think of me."

They stood there glaring at him for a moment and then walked off. They clearly didn't want to put into words what they thought of Tom. He continued up the other two flights of stairs to his room and let himself in. Sitting down on the edge of the bed, he cradled his head in his hands and began to sob quietly to himself.

Tom awoke in the middle of the night, because his bladder had sent an urgent message to his brain. He struggled out of bed and walked past the sink in his room on his way to the bathroom next door. It would save him quite a bit of effort if he used it as a urinal and for a moment, he was sorely tempted.

When a plumber is asked to install a sink in a hotel bedroom, he is always faced with the problem of how high to set it. This is because the guests in that room may be anywhere from very tall to very short. There is nothing worse than trying to wash yourself in a sink that is set so high that you have to stretch to reach it, or trying to use one that is set so low that you have to bend down to it.

Plumbers do appreciate this problem and as they

are also men of the world, they know that many men will use the sink in their hotel room as a urinal, to avoid having to traipse down the corridor to a toilet somewhere else in the building.

Accordingly, plumbers employ what is known as the 'knob rule', by which they stand next to where the sink is to be positioned and put a mark on the wall, at exactly the same height as the bottom of the zip in their trousers.

This gives the perfect placement, as long as your plumber is of average height. A tall plumber might leave you needing to resort to the 'fountain shot' (having to pee upwards like a fountain) and a short one would mean that you to have to pee straight downwards, which inevitably leads to splashing urine all over yourself.

Tom decided against using the sink and continued on to the toilet next door. He knew that he would want to use that sink in the morning, as he would need to wash his face, clean his teeth and have a shave before leaving the room.

When his radio alarm clock went off at half past seven, the song playing at the time was 'I Got You Babe' by Sonny and Cher. Anyone who has ever seen the film 'Groundhog Day' will know that this is the tune Bill Murray wakes up to every morning, when he keeps living the same day over and over again. The DJ on Tom's radio couldn't resist the temptation of quoting from the film, "OK, campers. Rise and shine," he shouted out, as the song finished.

Tom cursed him volubly and slowly crawled out of bed. Bill Murray's character used to meet a rather portly gentleman in the corridor each morning, who would gleefully wish him, "Happy Groundhog Day," every time. Tom knew that if he bumped into anyone like that he would probably kill them. For a moment, he considered the possibility that he was in a Groundhog Day situation, but then dismissed the thought. Things like that didn't happen in real life. Saturday was a day he would much rather forget. The last thing he needed was to have to live through it all again.

As he made his way down to breakfast (fortunately not meeting any chubby man with a death wish) he knew that the others would give him hell about peeing in the street. As it happened he was the first one down, so he found which table was theirs and sat down on his own. As he looked around, he saw the elderly couple from last night again. They were talking to the manager and he could see them repeatedly pointing in his direction.

"Oh, oh!" he said to himself. "I can see more trouble brewing." They were obviously telling the manager about what he had been up to in the early hours of the morning.

At that moment, the others came in and joined him. They all seemed quite cheerful and asked him how he felt after yesterday's excitement. "I've felt better," said Tom, but then noticed that the manager was heading their way. "I think I'm going to feel worse in a minute though."

The manager reached the table and addressed Tom directly, "What you did outside this hotel last night was disgusting," he began, "and I understand that you then started shouting and swearing when you did finally did come into the hotel."

The old couple had clearly given the manager the full details, so there was no point in denying it. "Guilty as charged," said Tom.

"He's got a prostate problem," George chimed in, "and he was only shouting outside our room to attract our attention. I don't recall him swearing at all though."

"Be that as it may," said the manager. "I don't think you four are the type of guests we want staying at this hotel. You have caused nothing but trouble since you first arrived and I would be far happier if you didn't come back. I'm very tempted to ask you to pack your suitcases and leave immediately, but I will allow you to eat breakfast first as a concession, seeing as how you have pre-paid for them."

"That is such a kind gesture," said Fred, very sarcastically.

"We're leaving today anyway," John told him. "So our bags are already packed and we just need to collect our meat from the hotel fridge. I don't think that we will want to stay here again anyway, as we don't like your attitude very much and would much rather stay in a place with a bar that actually opens occasionally."

"The hotel bar is open from noon every day of the

week other than Sunday," the manager protested. "It then stays open for a whole hour; although I do sometimes shut it early if there is no demand."

He stormed off when the four of them laughed in his face. The old couple Tom had upset were trying hard to pretend they weren't listening. They were both very shocked when all the boys turned in their direction simultaneously and gave them an evil grin.

One of the waiters came and took their orders and then winked broadly at them as he left. Clearly the manager wasn't popular with his staff either.

"I suppose I can find us a different hotel for next year," Fred said, "It shouldn't be too difficult."

"We won't worry about next year yet," George said. "This one's far from over and judging from what has happened to us over the last couple of days, our final day may be full of even more surprises."

After eating their breakfasts, they brought their bags down to the car and packed them in the boot, together with the meat from the hotel fridge. It was to be their last morning in Cromer and would turn out to be one that they would remember.

13

THE GAME OF BOWLS

Tom was pleased at the way his friends had rallied round him when the hotel manager was having his little tirade. He was almost prepared to forgive them for deserting him last night - but not quite.

John suggested that he had better shift the Jaguar out of the hotel car park and move it to one of the available parking places on the road. "I wouldn't put it past that twirp to complain to the police about me using his car park when we are no longer residents," he said, "and I don't want to give him the chance."

After he had moved the car, they discussed what they should do next. They knew that the crazy golf wouldn't open until ten thirty, so they had a bit of time to kill.

On one previous occasion, they had managed to have a go at bowling on the Cromer bowls green. They had simply asked whether they could and were very surprised when they were told that it would be okay. The club members there even provided them with a choice of different sizes of appropriate shoes from the club store, together with the bowls they would need, a mat and their own scoring board.

"They must be mad to let us four loose on their green," George had said at the time. "We don't know the first thing about bowls and I hate to think of the damage we might cause clod-hopping around." The surface of the green was as smooth as a billiard table and the lush green grass was finely trimmed to present a perfect playing area.

"They probably think we are experienced bowls players who are here in Cromer on holiday," Tom suggested. "We will have to be on our best behaviour and try not to make ourselves look like prats."

"That might be difficult, as we don't know what we're doing," George contributed, "but it can't really be that difficult, can it? It's only a game of marbles after all, but we just have to use bigger marbles."

If only life was as simple as that, but of course it's not. Underestimating situations like this can lead to disaster and history is littered with examples of people doing just that. One only has to look back at the Battle of Hastings. When King Harold was told that the Normans were advancing on his position and the troops asked him what they should do, he is reported to have said something to the effect of: "But they are still a long way away and are only firing little sticks up in the air. What possible harm could things like that do?"

When the Titanic ploughed into an iceberg and ripped a hole along its side below the waterline, a junior officer called Captain Smith up to the bridge and was probably told off for waking him up. Some accounts say that the captain actually said, "So we've bumped into a big lump of ice. So what? This ship is unsinkable, don't you know?"

George was making the same classic mistake, which effectively guaranteed that their game of bowls was going to end up as a fiasco.

Marbles are made very cheaply and look very pretty, with a little multi-coloured wave positioned in the centre. Bowls are manufactured to a very high standard and weight is added to one side to provide what is known as bias. This ensures that the bowl will follow a curved trajectory, depending on how it is held in the hand prior to release. Marbles are nothing like so complicated. You simply throw a marble and it goes in a straight line.

When a right-handed bowler holds his bowl so that the bias is on the left, he will roll it out to the right and as it begins to run out of steam, it will start curving in to the left. This is known as a forehand draw. If he reverses his grip of the bowl and bowls out to the left, the bowl then turns in to the right as it approaches the head (which is where all the other bowls and the jack are gathered). This is called a backhand draw. The opposite would apply to a left-hander. The bowler knows which side of his bowl is the one with bias, because a symbol inside the circle on it indicates that point. Accordingly, he knows exactly how to hold the bowl, in order to achieve the sort of shot he wants.

The boys were not completely ignorant about the game of bowls, as they had all watched it on television once or twice. They knew that you didn't aim straight for the jack, but rolled your bowl out in one direction or the other and that it would curve in afterwards. They understood that this happened because the bowls were heavier on one side and that this was called bias. They also knew that you stood on a mat as you released your bowl and that the idea was to get as close to the jack as you could. That is where the sum total of their knowledge of the game ended.

"How many bowls do we need?" John asked, as they all tried on different shoes in the clubhouse.

"Haven't got a clue," Tom told him. "How many are they using out there?" There were four members of the club playing a game at that time, so this was quite a sensible suggestion.

John went to the doorway and counted up how many bowls they were using. "They are playing with eight, so I guess that means we all have two each."

Fred was busy weighing up a bowl in his hand, by lifting it up and down. "How are we meant to know which side is heaviest?" he asked his fellow experts.

"I think there's a circle on them somewhere

which tells you," said George.

"This one's got a circle on both sides and there are different symbols in each of them," Fred pointed out, "so I don't see how that helps me."

"It will doubtless all make sense when we start playing," said Tom optimistically.

A short while later and they all marched out of the clubhouse, carrying their two sets of four bowls, the mat and the scoring board. They had managed to find reasonably comfortable shoes to fit everyone.

The club members were playing their game on the extreme right hand rink (the technical term for the strip of lawn on which they were bowling) so the boys decided that it would probably be safest if they went to the one on the opposite side of the green, so as to be as far away from them as possible.

"Don't drop the bowls down too heavily," said John. "We wouldn't want to dent the grass."

"Which way do we go?" Fred then wanted to know. "Should we start from here, or should we go up to the other end and start from there?"

They all stood thinking about this for a moment, before John said that he didn't think it mattered. "We have to play in both directions anyway," he told them, "so which end we actually start at can't be all that important."

It was decided to play a team game. No one knew what they were doing anyway, so Fred suggested that he and John should play as partners against

Tom and George. This was fine with the others so with the teams chosen, they were ready to make a start.

Someone had to send the jack (the target ball) up the rink, so they tossed a coin to decide who this should be. George and Tom won the toss and George was given the honour. He carefully placed the mat on the green and stood in the middle of it, holding the jack in his hand.

"Overarm or underarm?" he asked the others.

"Underarm, you idiot!" John shouted at him. "This is bowls, not cricket!"

George rolled the jack up the rink, but was rather surprised to see that it didn't even reach half way. "It's a lot further than it looks," he said. "Do we play with it there, or should I have another go?"

"Go and get it," Tom told him. "I'm sure it's meant to be further away than that."

George retrieved the jack and had another go. He threw it a lot harder this time and it rolled right off the far end of the rink and into the ditch. He walked off down the green to fetch it and then came back to try again.

"It is going to take hours at this rate," said Fred. "No one's even bowled yet and if it's going to be that hard just to position the jack, what the hell is it going to be like when we do start bowling?"

"Third time lucky," said George, as he threw the jack down the rink again.

It ended up near to where it was supposed to be and everyone agreed that this would have to do.

George stood on the mat with his first bowl in his hand. He looked at the symbols in the circles on both sides and made a guess as to which one indicated where the bowl was weighted. It was the wrong guess. He aimed to the left and expected to see the bowl swing back in. It travelled in a straight line and went off the green and into the ditch before it was even half way up the rink. "Oops!" said George.

It was now John's turn and he was faced with making the same decision. The symbol in one of the circles was bigger than the one on the other side, so it seemed logical that this indicated the heavier side. He held the bowl in his right hand, with what he hoped was the heavier side pointing to the left, and aimed to the right. He was attempting a forehand draw (see Page 111) but was holding the bowl the wrong way round. It shot off to the right and continued turning even further right as it went. It eventually came to rest more of less in the middle of the green, about the same distance from all four of its sides.

"I don't think that one is going to be a winner," Tom said with some amusement.

"Let's see you do better then," John retorted.

It was Tom's go next and when he asked John which way he had been holding his bowl, John told him to find out for himself. "You can't expect me to give you tips. You're on the opposing team."

Tom took a guess and guessed right. He aimed his bowl to the right and was overjoyed when it began to turn left after travelling some distance. The only problem was that it came to rest only two thirds of the way up the rink. His attempt was however the best so far.

Before Fred rolled his bowl, John gave him the wisdom of his experience and told him how to position the bowl in his hand. It was only after he had taken his shot that John realised the advice he had given him was wrong. Fred was left-handed and his bowl followed George's into the side ditch.

After a few more ends, they all finally worked out which way round to hold the bowl and were starting to achieve some success. They had decided to move over one rink after the first end, as Fred claimed that he was being seriously disadvantaged. He had no choice but to bowl with his left hand, which meant that it was almost impossible for him to avoid going into the ditch on the left hand side of the rink.

They all found it extremely difficult to judge how hard to roll their bowls and most fell short by quite a long way. A few were rolled too hard and ended up in the end ditch and several shot off across the green in the direction of the game being played by the club members. A few of them still managed to end up in the side ditch, irrespective of which side it was on.

Nobody managed to get anywhere near the jack, let alone coming to rest next to it, and deciding which of the bowls was nearest proved to be rather difficult as well. It might had been better had they brought a extra long extendable tape measure with them, as even some of their nearest bowls were often more than seven feet away.

After six ends, they decided that they'd had enough fun at bowls and that it was time to stop. It was impossible to say which team had actually won (because of the difficulty deciding which bowl was nearest) but they all agreed that they'd had a bloody good time and hadn't made too much of a fool of themselves.

As they walked past the club members on their way to return the borrowed equipment, one of them glanced over at them and said, "Hope you enjoyed the game, lads. Come back any time."

"Thank you very much," John told him. "We would definitely like to do that." They were all hoping that they had convinced these seasoned experts that they weren't complete novices at the game.

They knew they had failed when the man added, "You didn't do too badly for your first game!"

Every year since, they had always looked in at the bowls club whenever they were in Cromer, in the hope that there would be some members there who might let them have another go. There never did see anybody whenever they checked, so they only ever got to play that one game.

"We could walk over to the bowls club and see if there are any members around," Tom suggested, "while we are waiting for the crazy golf to open."

"Can you just imagine what reaction we'd get

after me banging a golf ball into the middle of one of their matches yesterday?" John asked him.

"Oh, yes," said Tom. "I had forgotten all about that for a moment."

14

TOM SAVES THE DAY

They were standing on the pavement opposite the hotel, next to the path that cut through the putting green, when a car pulled up and a couple of guys dashed into the hotel. They didn't pay that much attention until they came out again with the manager, who glanced around before pointing out the boys to the men with him.

"What do you suppose that's about?" John asked the others.

"Looks like we are about to find out," said George, as the two men ran across the road towards them.

"Are you the four blokes who foiled the jewellery store robbery last night?" one of them enquired.

"We might be," John answered. "Why do you want to know?" He didn't know what was going on and didn't want to commit himself.

The two men introduced themselves as reporters from the local paper. They had heard all about the attempted robbery and having discovered where the boys were staying, had rushed over to the hotel to interview them.

"We want to do a feature article for next week's paper," one of them said. "It's not every day that things like that happen in Cromer, so we will make a big thing of it, with pictures of the four of you. We'd like to get some of you outside the jewellers and may even have you pose with this year's Miss Cromer."

"I don't think Miss Cromer would care for that idea very much," Tom commented.

"Whatever," said the reporter. "Now tell us what you are doing here and what you've been up to."

They explained that this was their boy's weekend in Cromer and that they came here every year to play different competitive events and to see the End of the Pier Show. The reporter was very keen to hear what sort of competitions they meant and when they told him, he immediately began to scribble furiously in the notebook he was carrying. "This is great!" he said. "The readers are really going to love all this. I've never heard of rock pool petanque before."

"Did you go to see last night's show on the pier?" the other reporter asked. "Apparently, some poor sod in the audience got picked on and was called a dirty old lecher?"

"Yes, we were there," George told him, "and we thought the show was thoroughly enjoyable."

There was no way that Tom was going to admit

to being the dirty old lecher in question, so he kept quiet and hoped the others wouldn't drop him in it.

"We'd like to meet that bloke," the second reporter continued, "particularly if he is the one who caught the golden crab."

The other three looked at Tom, who appeared to have suddenly developed an all-consuming interest in one of the pansies planted in a bed on the wall next to him. He'd already been embarrassed enough for one weekend, so they decided to keep quiet.

They continued talking to the reporters for another quarter of an hour or so, during which time they posed for several photographs. John gave an account of what had happened in the jewellery shop, but neglected to make any mention of him claiming to be a major in the SAS.

"There is bound to be a reward, you know," one of the reporters said. "You will all have to come back to Cromer for its presentation. You may even be given the freedom of the town. We will get the mayor to attend and also the entire cast of the End of the Pier Show. Loads of pictures will be taken and the story might even be picked up by some of the national newspapers."

The reporters were clearly very excited about their scoop and Fred needed to point out that they were on a tight schedule for their last day in Cromer and that they had a game of crazy golf to play.

It was with some reluctance that the reporters finally left and the boys watched them call in at the hotel again before getting in their car and driving off.

What happened next took them all by surprise, as they thought they'd said their final goodbye to the hotel manager. He suddenly appeared at the front door and rushed across the road to speak to them.

"I can only apologise for that misunderstanding this morning," he blurted out. "If I had known what you went through last night and how you had to face armed robbers in that shop, I would never have spoken to you in the way I did. I didn't know that you are all heroes and the hotel is indeed lucky to have four such brave men staying with us."

The boys all looked at each other. They hadn't expected this and were highly amused to see his obvious discomfort at having to apologise to them.

"You are of course welcome to come back any time and I will make sure that you are given our very best rooms," he blathered on, "and if you could mention our hotel when you are being interviewed, then you will not find me ungrateful."

"We will certainly tell the press how you treat the guests in your hotel," George told him. "It will be our pleasure, although you may not like what we have to say. With regard to staying at your hotel again, I think I will leave it to Tom to answer that one."

Tom looked at the manager and said, "Thank you very much for your very kind invitation, but get stuffed!"

The manager looked a bit stunned. He wasn't

such a bad bloke really, but the pressures of running a hotel had worn him down over the years and he tended to have his occasional Basil Faulty moments. He slowly walked away and returned to the hotel.

It still wasn't quite ten thirty, so they strolled over to the open sided seafront shelter on the path along the cliff top. It's a very pleasant place to sit and relax (providing it's not too windy) and watch all the joggers, dog walkers and all the other people using the path go by.

John walked over to the railings by the side of the path and looked down at the beach far below, where children were running about flying kites. "We've never thought about including kite flying in our weekend," he casually mentioned to the others. "It's something we might think about for next year."

"There are enough things to try and fit in as it is," Fred responded, "and I wouldn't want to stand there flying a kid's toy at my age. That would make me look really stupid."

"That's exactly what you said last year," George pointed out, "when Tom suggested that we have a go at canoe racing round the boating lake. I'm starting to think you're turning into an old stick-in-the-mud and don't want to do things just for fun anymore."

"I wore plus fours and silly socks for the pitch and putt match last year," Fred told him. "So don't tell me I've lost my sense of humour."

"You only did that to poke fun at me and George," John countered, "just because we take out golf fairly seriously. But you did look a right proper Charlie!"

They all chuckled as they remembered the sight of Fred in his golfing outfit and the look of utter disbelief on sixties man's face.

"Let's walk along the cliff path to town," suggested John. "There may still be some fresh cooked crabs for sale and I'd like to take one home with me."

"What is it with you and crustaceans?" Tom asked. "You wouldn't happen to be thinking about buying a plateful of whelks as well, would you? You can't need to get whelked-up now, not after having eaten most of that huge breakfast."

"I never said anything about buying whelks," John said. "I just want to see if I can get a crab."

"If you'd had said something earlier," Tom told him, "then we might have put a bit more effort into not allowing the golden crab I caught yesterday to escape." They began strolling towards the town.

Above their heads, a hang-glider was wheeling and swooping about in the sky. "You can't call that a children's toy, Fred," George said. "We could always . . ."

"Don't even think about it!" Fred quickly answered.

The hang-glider looked as if it was beginning to descend and the boys decided to stop and watch it. There was a large patch of lawn next to them, between the path and the main road, and this was probably what the hang-glider pilot was aiming for.

The huge multi-coloured sail swooped this way and that, losing height all the time as it did so, and they were all impressed by the skill with which it was being handled. The pilot then turned it into the wind above the putting course and started to glide in. It would have been a textbook landing, but for the sudden gust of crosswind that caught the sail at the moment before touchdown.

The hang-glider was slammed sideways, to crash into the railings guarding the path along the cliff top. It became entangled and the wing collapsed, as the air spilt out of it. The boys watched in horror as it hung there right on the edge for a moment, with its framework precariously hooked on the railing. The pilot was trapped beneath the wrecked craft and it was a very long way down to the promenade below.

Everyone nearby just stood there in shock, but Tom acted on impulse and dashed forward to try to prevent the hang-glider breaking loose and plunging down the cliff, together with its pilot.

He grabbed hold of the framework and hung on for all he was worth. The others rushed over to help and when it looked as if everyone had a tight grip, Tom leaned over the railing and stretched down to try and reach the pilot's hand. The full crash helmet did not stop him seeing the look of abject terror in the pilot's eyes and he redoubled his efforts. He had now leaned over so far that the others had to hang on to him as well, but he finally managed to grab hold of a waving hand and slowly began to pull the pilot up.

When facing tension or extreme anxiety, a sudden burst of adrenalin into a person's bloodstream can give them what appears to be superhuman strength. It certainly seemed that way to Tom, because the pilot felt as light as a feather. He continued pulling and a minute or so later, a slim helmeted figure was standing next to him and shaking like a leaf.

"Are you all right?" Tom asked urgently, as he helped remove the crash helmet. The long cascading curls of golden hair concealed the girl's face for a moment, but then she looked up, straight into Tom's eyes. It was none other than Miss Cromer!

She threw her arms around his neck and burst into tears. Tom turned as red as a beetroot. All the others were far too stunned to say anything, so they just stood there looking lost.

Miss Cromer continued hanging on to Tom's neck for a good five minutes, while she tried to regain her composure. Violent sobs were wracking her body and Tom, not knowing what else to do, was gently patting her back in a fatherly fashion.

She finally recovered enough to let go of him and John pulled out a handkerchief which he gave the girl, so that she could wipe away her tears.

She looked at each of them in turn and then her eyes returned to Tom. "I just don't know what to say to you," she told him. "You just saved my life and now I feel absolutely beastly about what I said about you in the theatre last night."

George was very tempted to say, "He probably would have dropped you had he known who you were," but then thought better of it.

Tom looked sheepish. "Even dirty old men have been known to do good deeds occasionally," he said, which only made her burst into tears again.

By now the police had turned up and the sergeant (inevitably the same one) saw who was gathered there and said, "Oh no! I don't believe it. It's you four again."

"Sorry if we are taking up too much of your time, sergeant," Fred quipped.

The remains of the hang-glider were separated from the railings and dumped on the patch of lawn. "We will get somebody to come along with a van to pick that lot up later," one of the policemen said. "We had better run you over to the hospital for a check up Miss, if you would like to come with us now."

She looked across at Tom and then rushed over to hug him again. "You're my hero," she told him, "and I don't even know your name."

"It's Tom, Tom Edwards," he blurted out with some difficulty. He felt embarrassed to be called a hero.

"Well, Tom Edwards, my name is Jenny Brown and I really would like you to be my friend. Please give me your phone number and e-mail address, as I can't let you walk out of my life for me never to see you again - and I do want to see you again."

Fred handed him a pen and a piece of paper and he wrote them down, before passing the sheet to Jenny. She tore it in half and wrote her own contact details on the second part, before giving this back to Tom. As she began walking towards the police car, she suddenly stopped and ran back. Tom was amazed when she gave him the biggest wet kiss he'd ever had. All he could say afterwards was, "Wow!"

After Jenny and the police had left, John turned to Tom and said, "Well, you've always said that one day you'll get lucky and I think today is that day. You've obviously made a really big impression on that girl and I rather suspect that you intend to see a lot more of Miss Cromer."

"Providing you lot don't rat on me to Deidre," Tom answered with a big grin.

"Are we ever going to play crazy golf?" asked Fred. "Or are any of you planning on finding other ways to disrupt my schedule?"

15

GOLF CAN BE A CRAZY GAME

The course was already set out when they reached it and they were not surprised to see that the order in which they needed to play the holes was just as confusing as ever. This was mostly due to the fact that the painted hole numbers on the various obstacles had worn off years ago, leaving one having to guess as to which obstacle belonged to what hole.

On one occasion, they had just completed the seventh, only to find that the next obstacle on the course had the number four on it. To avoid such problems in the future, they had taken to walking the course first, just to make sure they knew where all the holes were positioned.

The first thing they noticed was that the playing card obstacle still hadn't been stabilised or replaced. It was about forty inches high by twenty four inches wide and represented the ace of clubs. It was about six inches wide and there were matching holes at the base, both front and back. The player needed to putt through these holes from directly in front, or the ball would get trapped inside with no way of getting it back out again, other than actually picking the thing up. The specific problem with this obstacle was its lack of stability. The slightest puff of wind would blow it over, which didn't help if you were in the middle of trying to putt a ball through it. The boys had asked for something to be done about it several times, but it was still there again this year, just waiting for a slight breeze to knock it down.

Another obstacle which always made them laugh was the spider. Its head was in the shape of a dome and the gaps between its legs formed small arches through which you had to putt your ball. You went in through one arch and hoped to come out through one on the other side.

Generally speaking, spiders have eight legs, but whoever designed this one obviously didn't know that, as Cromer's spider only has six legs. This means that if you putt directly through one of the holes in its base, your ball will hit one of the legs directly opposite. This would not happen if it was a standard eight-legged spider - as simple geometry can prove.

The result is that balls almost always get stuck in the middle and the boys had to resort to lying on the grass and using their putters as billiard cues, to try and pott the ball between the legs on the opposite side. They didn't know whether this was allowed in the rules of the game, but it was the only solution they had managed to come up with.

Their game had therefore become a combination of putting and potting and this being the case; they couldn't see why this shouldn't be extended to allow other shots from billiards, like cannons. A cannon is where a player deliberately aims to collide with another player's ball, with the intention of moving it to promote the position of his own ball. It is a bit more complicated than that, but an example will illustrate the point.

Several of the obstacles on the Cromer crazy golf course have ramps leading up to them, which your ball has to be driven up, in order to pass through the obstacle. It is very rare that a ball ever gets putted straight up the ramp from the tee position, as the clumpy grass and bare patches of earth make such precision targeting impossible. The way to cope with the problem is to try and putt your ball to end up somewhere near the approach to the ramp, so that it becomes a far easier target for your next shot. This is where cannons come into it, as the opposing player will aim straight at your ball and try to knock it away from the ramp, while leaving his own closer to it.

The boys had worked very hard at perfecting this technique and purposely going for an opponent's ball, rather than aiming to get through the obstacle, was now considered to be a legitimate shot.

"This discarded cigarette packet will mark the position for the first tee," said George, as they stood there with their putters, waiting to begin the final competition of this year's Cromer weekend. Tom was his partner and he was concerned that Tom still seemed to be floating on cloud nine, after his extremely exhilarating snogging session with Miss Cromer.

"You will need to concentrate on the game Tom," he told him. "You know how important it is that we win this one."

"I know, I know," said Tom. "It's just that I can't get the thought of that kiss out of my mind. She really did kiss me passionately."

John looked at Fred and commented, "I think we're going to win easily today."

Play began and George aimed for the first obstacle, which was humpty dumpty sitting on a wall. His ball was directly on target until it hit a dog-end on the ground and was deflected off in totally the wrong direction.

John followed and managed to miss the dog-end. His ball came to rest a few feet short of Humpty Dumpty, which meant that he had a very good chance of putting through one of the tunnels at the base of the wall with his next shot.

"It's your go Tom," George had to tell him. Tom was absent-mindedly staring into space, but he came back down to earth for a moment to take his shot. His ball bounced this way and that on its erratic path to the obstacle and actually stopped in the mouth of one of Humpty Dumpty's tunnels.

"I don't believe that shot!" said John. "You never

normally play that well."

The game continued and it looked as if Tom's run of good luck was not going to leave him just yet. Even when he missed what he was aiming for, he still seemed to get lucky.

On the fifth hole, both John and George's balls were positioned just short of the ramp and it would be John's turn to go first, after Tom had taken his shot. Tom's ball smacked into George's and his partner's ball shot straight up the ramp. It passed through the obstacle (which bore some resemblance to a tower block) and dropped straight into the hole when it exited on the other side.

"Nice one," said George. They had won four out of the first five holes and if the game continued the way it was going, they were likely to end up winning by the biggest margin ever.

On the ninth hole, Tom was staring up into the sky again and George needed to remind him that it was his turn to play. "Wake up Tom," he said. "Stop your daydreaming and try to concentrate on the game."

"I wasn't daydreaming," Tom told him. "I was just watching that helicopter."

They all looked up to see the huge shape of the bright yellow Air Ambulance circling in the sky. It was not directly above them but as they watched, it began to turn towards them until it was immediately above their heads.

There are not that many places to land a helicopter near the town itself and the crazy golf course is one of the possible options. It is bordered on three sides by buildings, but is quite a large and moderately flat area of grass. The lawn near the cliff top path would be another, but the remains of Jenny's hang-glider were still sitting right in the middle of it.

It quickly became clear that the pilot intended to land on the course, as one of the crew could be seen furiously waving at the boys below, as if to say, "Get out the way!" (or words to that effect).

As the helicopter began its descent, all the light obstacles round the course were blasted away like pieces of confetti and Humpty Dumpty went flying past John's ear as the boys all ran for cover. Even the little hut which hires out all the putting clubs and balls was blown over onto its side. The noise level was deafening and everyone felt that their ear drums were being assaulted. The force of the downdraft turned the surface of the boating lake into a maelstrom, with canoeists diving overboard to seek the comparative safety of the shallow water.

The disturbance lasted for no more than two minutes, by which time the helicopter was safely down on the ground and its rotors were beginning to slowly wind down.

A couple of crewmen leapt out carrying equipment and ran off in the direction of town. The boys got up from where they had been lying on the ground and brushed themselves off. This was a real emergency happening in front of their eyes and they were interested to find out what was going on.

Another crewman stepped out from the helicopter and walked over to where they were standing. "I'm sorry if we messed up your game," he said, "but we had nowhere else to land. Some idiot has parked their hang-glider on the only other place we could have used." He went on to explain that a man in the ice cream parlour had suffered a heart attack and obviously needed urgent attention. The ambulance hadn't been able to get through the town because of a coach outside the Hotel Splendide, so they had answered the call as they happened to be in the area.

After they had been talking for a while, they noticed that the other two crew members were now returning. They didn't seem to be in that much of a hurry. "Were we too late to save him?" the crewman shouted at them, with concern in his voice.

"No," one of them replied. "It was a false alarm. He hadn't had a heart attack after all. The only thing wrong with him was a case of chronic indigestion, probably caused by the ice cream he was eating."

"Was it rum and raisin?" Fred enquired.

The crewman was astonished. "How did you know that?" he asked.

"I always get bad indigestion whenever I eat rum and raisin ice cream," Fred told him.

They all laughed about that and the boys were allowed on board the helicopter so that they could see all the equipment inside, before it lifted off again and peace and quiet returned to the area.

The young girl in charge of the crazy golf course was standing next to her hut, looking at all the shambles inside. The crew from the helicopter and the boys had helped turn it back on its base, but it now seemed to be leaning at a bit of an odd angle.

All the various obstacles from the course were now scattered everywhere and one could even be seen perched on the balcony of one of the apartments which overlooked the green.

"How do you feel about going to ask if we can have our obstacle back, John?" said Tom.

"Not a chance," he replied. "I don't want to take the chance of them throwing me off the balcony!"

They had only managed to play the first eight holes and Tom and George had won six of them. It didn't now look as if they would be able to continue with the game, so it was decided that it should be abandoned, with Tom and George being declared the winners. Fred wasn't terribly happy about this, as he considered that his team could have caught up and overtaken them, had they been able to play the full eighteen holes.

"Now you're just being a bad loser," George told him. "You never would have beaten us anyway, not the way my partner was playing."

It was now nearly half past eleven and they knew that the live jazz band at the King's Arms, Reepham would start playing at midday. They didn't usually get there before one, which meant they caught the last hour or so. Reepham was less than twenty miles away, so there was no rush to leave just yet.

"Well," said John. "We've got a little bit of time on our hands, so let's make Fred's day and straighten up his ruined schedule."

"What do you mean?" asked Fred.

"I mean," continued John, "that we have time to go over to the community club to start on those games of singles pool. We won't be able to play all of them, but at least it will mean that we've had a go at all the different events you've got on your schedule."

"It would tidy things up a bit," Fred admitted.

John suggested that they walk over there and make a start, while he went to get the Jaguar. He would then park it close to the community club, so they could then drive straight to Reepham from there.

As the three of them were walking to the club, Tom asked Fred whether he had any ideas about where they might stay next year.

"I thought we might try the Hotel Splendide," he suggested. The room rates there are reasonable and we'd fit right in, now that we are all getting older."

"That place is just like God's waiting room," exclaimed Tom. "There's no way I'd consider staying there."

But some of the guests bring their own private nurses with them and there are bound to be some pretty ones amongst them," Fred told him.

"What do I care about that?" Tom responded with

a big smile. "I've got my Miss Cromer!"

They had time to play three games of pool before they needed to leave. Tom's luck appeared to have finally deserted him, as he didn't win either of the games he took part in.

All too soon, it was time to say goodbye to Cromer for another year and they all walked back to the car. Their last morning here had certainly been eventful, as had the entire weekend, but there was still the jazz to look forward to and their next visit was only a year away. They all knew that Tom wouldn't be able to stay away for that long, not with Miss Hot Lips Jenny waiting for him. But then he would need to come up by train as he didn't drive. They didn't think he'd considered that point yet.

16

HOMEWARD BOUND

As they drove out of town on the A149, they were all reflecting on everything that had happened over the weekend. Fred was happy, because it had more of less followed his schedule, apart from not playing all the singles pool games and Tom was sitting there in the back of the car with a great big grin on his face.

"So what are you going to tell Deidre when you want to sneak up to Cromer again to see Jenny?" George asked him.

"I don't know yet," Tom replied, "but I will probably think of something."

"You do appreciate, I take it," shouted John over his shoulder, "that when Jenny's calmed down after that terrifying ordeal, she will realise that her hero is still just a dirty old man? She might not be quite so keen on you when she starts thinking rationally again. If you do contact her, I wouldn't mind betting that you will get quite a cool reception."

"Possibly," said Tom, "but I almost certainly saved her life, so she will want to show her appreciation to me in some way or another."

"She will probably give you her grandmother's phone number," Fred chipped in.

"Mock all you like, you're just jealous. I was the one she snogged. None of you lot got as much as a peck on the cheek!"

"I suppose you might get that night out on the town with her, as the golden crab competition winner," John commented, "but that's probably all you'll get."

"I hope the rest of the prize is not a holiday at that hotel where we've been staying," Tom said, as he began to think about what else he might have won. "Now that would be really embarrassing."

The journey continued and they didn't see any policemen waving them down, let alone any broken down monster trucks or escaped chimpanzees. They joined the A140 heading towards Aylsham, where they turned off onto the minor road which went to Reepham. Most of the conversation in the car now revolved around trying to remember some of the jokes they'd heard at the End of the Pier Show.

The sun was shining and it was a lovely day. They'd had a really good weekend, which was something they would enjoy talking about for weeks at the Nag's Head. After everything else that had happened, they felt sure that there couldn't possibly be any more surprises in store for them.

They hadn't been on the minor road for very long when they came across a man standing in the middle of the road. He looked dishevelled and was waving his arms around in an extremely agitated fashion.

"There aren't any lunatic asylums anywhere near here, are there?" asked Fred, "because he looks as if he might have just escaped from one."

"We will have to stop," John told them. "The road isn't wide enough for me to drive round him." He brought the car to a halt just short of the crazy looking man, who immediately ran to John's side of the car and began banging on his window furiously. John had thought it prudent to close it before he stopped the car. He pressed a button to lower the window by an inch or so, just so that he would be able to hear what the wild man had to say.

"You stopped!" the frantic lunatic shouted, which seemed to be a really stupid thing to say.

"You didn't give me much choice," John retorted. "It was that or run you over."

"My wife is having a baby!" the man yelled out excitedly.

"Congratulations!" John responded.

"No!" said the man. "You don't understand. I mean that my wife is having her baby right now!"

His agitation suddenly made more sense to them and the boy's realised that there had to be a problem with his wife being about to give birth.

They all jumped out of the car and John asked

him to explain himself slowly and clearly.

"My wife has gone into labour," he told them, "and when I went to start the car to drive her to hospital, the damn thing wouldn't start."

"Why didn't you ring for an ambulance then?" Fred asked him.

"Because this is Norfolk and you can never get a bloody signal anywhere round here."

Fred quickly glanced at his mobile, which was showing a whole line of empty spaces, where he would normally expect to see five bars. He had no signal either.

"What about your land line?" Tom suggested.

"That doesn't work either," the man told him. "The farmer next door cut through the buried lead when he was ploughing a couple of weeks ago and British Telecom hasn't got around to repairing it yet."

"How can we help?" asked John.

It was obvious that they needed to get the car to the woman in the first instance so they all piled back in, with the expectant father in the front passenger seat. He indicated a narrow opening in the hedge and told John that he would need to drive through it.

It wasn't so much a road as a narrow farm track and it was not only very rutted, but there were huge potholes everywhere as well. John drove as carefully as he possibly could.

After having travelled a few hundred yards along it, they met a stream crossing the path. It looked like it was only about a foot deep and had to be passable, if it was meant to be a ford. "That's why I'm in such a mess," the man told them. "I tripped over and fell in when I ran across it to get to the road." They could see a house about fifty yards further on.

John entered the ford very slowly and was very nearly across when a submerged pothole made its presence known. The car suddenly dropped to one side as a front wheel went straight into it and there was an almighty cracking sound, as something important broke. John tried to move forward, but the car wouldn't respond. "I think we've broken a drive shaft," he told the others. "We're not going be going anywhere if that is what's happened."

There was nothing for it but to get out of the car and they all had to wade across the ford to reach the other side. The man dashed off towards his house, while the others glanced down at their soaking wet trainers and trousers legs before following him.

At the house, it became immediately apparent that the woman was in the very later stages of labour and that it was now far too late to consider taking her anywhere, even if they had any transport to do so. The husband was busy trying to comfort her and she was moaning in anguish, as each fresh spasm hit her. "Do any of you know how to deliver a baby?" he asked in desperation, "because there is no one else around and I don't think it's going to be long before she bursts."

The boys all looked at each other with totally

blank expressions. Despite their ages, none of them had a clue about what happens when a baby gets born and even John, who had a son of his own, had chickened out of attending his birth - which might well have given him some insight into what actually went on.

The woman was lying on the sofa in the lounge and groaned even more when she saw their reaction. There was nothing for it now. She was in the hands of four older men who obviously didn't know what they were doing and a husband who was now falling to pieces in front of her eyes.

The surrogate midwives all dashed into the kitchen to wash their hands. They knew enough to know that this was important. They then started looking around for towels and linen, after Fred had said that he thought those sorts of things were always needed when someone was giving birth.

"How do we get ourselves into these situations?" Tom asked, as he searched a cupboard in the kitchen for anything that might be suitable.

A few minutes later and they had carried the woman through to the dining room and made her as comfortable as possible on the table in there. It was possibly not the best place to try and deliver a baby, but there was more room there than on the sofa.

George had mentioned that surgeons always wore masks, so each of them secured a handkerchief to cover the lower half of their faces, held in place by a couple of rubber bands stretched around the back of their necks. They may not have known what they were doing, but they did at least look the part.

Delivery a baby turned out to be easier than they thought, although it was a lot messier than they had expected. They were all confused when they found that the baby was still attached to the mother by its umbilical cord, but when the placenta plopped out after the baby, everything seemed to be as it was meant to be and they stopped panicking.

The baby was a boy and from the amount of noise he immediately began making, there didn't seem to be that much wrong with him. He appeared strong and healthy and after hc had been wrapped up in a number of tea towels, a very emotional George handed him over to the mother. She looked totally physically drained, but didn't look half as bad as the delivery team. The husband had been of no help whatsoever, so John had sent him back to the lounge, to get him out of the way during the actual birth. He now returned to the dining room and gazed proudly at his wife and their new son.

"I just don't know what to say," he told them. "I was totally useless there and you guys stepped in and took over. It's all thanks to you that everything went so well and I don't know what would have happened if you hadn't been here."

"We wouldn't have been here at all if you hadn't stopped us," Tom told him. "We would have been listening to a live jazz band in Reepham." It was now after two in the afternoon, so they had missed the concert.

The new mother also thanked them profusely and

asked for their names. She was going to have her new son christened with the names of the four men who had brought him into the world. After they had told her, she lay there repeating each name in turn for a minute or two.

"John, Thomas, Frederick, George Mulligan," she said. "I think it has a nice ring to it."

"You may need to revise the order a bit," George suggested. "I really don't suppose your son will appreciate being called John Thomas."

They were now stranded just outside the village of Cawston in Norfolk with no transport, a car that had broken down and no signals on their phones. Fred's schedule had been blown out of the water, but he didn't appear to be all that concerned about it. He seemed to be more taken with just staring at the newly born child.

They knew that the new mother and baby would need to be checked over by someone who did know what they were doing, so one of them would have to walk to the nearby village for help. They discussed who this should be, but eventually decided that they would all go.

Having made sure that the woman and baby were comfortable (they had been moved back to the sofa by now) and making sure that the husband wasn't about to have another panic attack, they set off. As their shoes were now beginning to dry out, having been left outside in the sun for a while, they didn't want to get them wet again, so waded across the ford in their bare feet with their trousers rolled up.

Cawston is not a particularly large village, but it does have a pub and a church. St Agnes church is famous for its painted rood screen and the fact that it has one of the earliest examples of a double hammer-beam roof in the country. For this reason, the village does get quite a few visitors.

The boys reached the pub just as it was closing at three, but when they explained that they were only late because they'd had to stop to deliver a baby, the landlord served them anyway and wanted to know the full story. The young couple with the new baby were known in the village, as they both visited the pub from time to time, so he telephoned a nurse who lived in the village and asked her to pop along and see them.

"Tell her she won't be able to drive through the ford," John told the landlord. "I'm afraid my car is blocking it at the moment and will need a tow truck for it to be moved."

"We can soon sort that out," said the landlord. He went and spoke to one of the locals who was still sitting in the bar, hoping to get served another drink. "Harry is going to take his tractor and low-loader out to your car and bring it back to the pub car park," he told John a few minutes later. "It won't take long."

"That's great," said John. "I can give my local Jag dealers a call in the morning and get them to pick it up from here. I can't do anything about it now as they don't work on Sundays."

The landlord glanced up at the clock, which was

showing that it was well after closing time. "Oh, to hell with licensing hours," he said. "The bar's open again if anyone wants another drink." All the locals in the pub made a quick dash for the counter.

"Aren't you worried about the police finding out?" asked Tom. "You could possibly lose your license."

"I shouldn't think so," the landlord told him. "The local copper is the first one in that queue at the bar."

The boys settled down for another pint. They felt that they certainly deserved it, after what they had just been called on to do.

17

BEWARE THE SKY

"So what do we do now?" asked George. "We are stuck in Cawston without a car and it is forty odd miles home from here."

"We could obviously call a taxi," John said, "and then transfer the luggage into it and go . . ."

The others all looked up when John paused. Some thought had obviously just crossed his mind and they waited to hear what was coming.

John got up and walked over to the bar to have a word with the landlord. When he returned, he had a smile on his face.

"Or alternatively . . ." he said. "We could spend the night in Cawston and go home tomorrow. The chaps from the garage will be coming here to fetch my car, so we could get a lift back with them. I was thinking that this would give us an opportunity to call in on young John Thomas tomorrow morning, to see how he is getting on."

"Where will we find somewhere to stay?" asked

Fred, worrying about the organisational aspects.

"We could stay right here in this pub," John told them. "They have three double rooms and do bed and breakfast."

"I certainly don't want to share a bed with any of you lot," Tom commented.

"Don't worry Tom," John said, with a laugh. "Two of them are twin rooms, so we would all have a bed of our own. It will only cost £35.00 each and that's with breakfast as well."

"That sounds like a good idea to me," commented George, answering straight away, "I wouldn't mind visiting the little fellow tomorrow, to see how he is getting on."

With the decision made, John and Tom both used the public phone in the bar to call their wives and let them know that the weekend was going to be extended by another day. Tom needed John to speak to Deidre, to convince her that he wasn't spending the night with some woman he'd picked up. She was extremely suspicious, as this was just the sort of excuse he would use if he wanted sneak another night away with some bird.

John agreed to pick up the tab for their extra night and when the others argued about this, he pointed out that it was his fault that they were in this fix to begin with, as he was the one who had driven the car into a pothole.

Harry returned a while later and told them that the Jaguar was now in the car park. This meant that they had access to their luggage and the items they would need for their extra overnight stay.

All the other customers had left by now, but Harry was treated to a pint, which he took outside to drink. John suddenly realised that he should have offered him something for going to get the car and spoke to the landlord about it.

"I wouldn't bother too much about that," the landlord told him. "He's already feeling guilty enough about everything."

John didn't understand, so asked him to explain.

"None of this would have happened had the young couple been able to call for an ambulance," he said. "Harry is the prat who ploughed up their phone line and caused them to be disconnected!"

John paid for their rooms and they fetched what they needed from the car. Having taken everything upstairs, they returned to the bar to discuss what to do next. The landlord had long since finished serving and had locked the front door of the pub.

"It's a shame it's Sunday opening hours," George commented. "I could really do with another pint."

The landlord overheard him and came over and asked them whether they would like another drink.

"But, you're shut, aren't you?" George asked him.

"Yes. I'm shut to the general public," he replied, "but you four are residents now, so you can have whatever you want to drink whenever you want."

"Four pints of your best bitter then, please," George told him. He knew that he didn't need to ask the others whether they wanted one."

The Dutch smugglers were convinced that this shipment of cocaine would get through without any problems, because they had used the system eight times previously and it had worked flawlessly every time. Their inside man on the maintenance team at Schiphol Airport would conceal the drugs inside the wing space into which the aeroplane's undercarriage retracted, where it would remain safely hidden until their man at Norwich Airport could retrieve it after the plane had landed.

That man in the team worked in baggage handling, so it was easy for him to briefly climb up into the wing space unobserved. The package would then be added to all the suitcases and bags being unloaded from the plane, but this package would never reach the carousel where the passengers reclaimed their baggage. It would be spirited away long before that and the smugglers could then sit back and enjoy the fruits of their labours, when the drugs hit the streets of various different English cities.

The flight from Schiphol to Norwich only takes about fifty minutes and who was likely to pay that much attention to such a short inter-city flight on a quiet Sunday afternoon. Norwich Airport was the perfect choice, as it was in the middle of rural Norfolk and nothing exciting ever happened there.

While the boys were wading through the stream (on their way to the pub) the Dutch maintenance man securely taped a package to an inside surface within the wing. He was using Gorilla tape, as every advert he had ever seen said that it was the best. Once he was satisfied that it was secure, he walked away from the plane, totally confident that the ten kilos of cocaine would remain attached to where he had left it for the short duration of the flight.

The KLM flight from Schiphol to Norwich generally passes over the English coast at Happisburgh, which is about half way between Great Yarmouth and Cromer. A bit of low level turbulence meant that the pilot had to alter course slightly and the aeroplane actually crossed the English coast at Cromer. From there he could fly directly to Norwich, a straight run which would pass right over Cawston.

Cawston is about ten miles from Norwich Airport as the crow flies, so this was the point at which the pilot decided to lower the plane's undercarriage. It descended and locked into position without a hitch, but the slight turbulence the plane had experienced during the flight caused the drugs package to come loose. It would seem that Gorilla tape perhaps has its limitations after all. The ten kilos of cocaine dropped out of the plane and began plummeting to earth.

Newton's Law of Gravity states that any object in freefall will accelerate at the rate of thirty-two feet per second, per second, which can be translated into a terminal velocity in excess of one hundred and thirty miles per hour, when an object falling from a thousand feet up approaches the ground. This just happened to be the plane's height when its pilot decided to lower the undercarriage.

Ignoring Newton for a moment, the drugs package also had forward momentum, because of the speed of the aircraft at the moment it actually fell out. The combination of these two factors meant that the parcel of cocaine was travelling rather quickly and at a slight angle as it approached Cawston. John's Jaguar was parked directly along its line of trajectory.

When the package crashed into the base of the car's windscreen, it disintegrated as it punched a large hole through the screen itself. The toughened glass of car windscreens is meant to withstand the impact of fair sized stones, providing they hit it at a moderate speed. They are not designed to withstand ten kilograms of cocaine smashing into it at one hundred and thirty miles per hour.

The boys were playing petanque at the time. They had discovered that the pub had a pitch in the back garden and having grabbed their multi-coloured plastic boules from the car, were in the middle of playing a game. Fred's boule landed at exactly the same moment as the pack of cocaine hit the car's windscreen. The sound it made took them all by surprise. Plastic boules weren't meant to sound like that when they landed on a gravel surface. They all looked around, but couldn't immediately see what had happened.

"What have you put into that boule of yours?" Tom asked. "They surely aren't meant to sound like that when they hit the ground?"

Fred was just as mystified as everyone else, but then happened to glance over in the direction of where John's Jaguar was parked in the car park. The whole car seemed to be enveloped in what looked like a huge cloud of white something.

"John . . ." he said. "I think we should go and have a look at your car."

They rushed over and stared at the car in disbelief. Every square of the inside was covered in a thick layer of white dust.

The landlord rushed out of the pub having heard the loud noise and joined the boys by the Jaguar. "What the hell hit it?" he asked, but nobody could enlighten him. He stepped forward and dabbed a finger in the white dust, before gently touching it to his tongue.

"Bloody hell!" he shouted. "It's coke!"

A short time later, the baggage handler at Norwich Airport climbed up into the wheel space of an aircraft which had recently landed. He searched everywhere, but could only find a few bits of Gorilla tape. There was no sign of the package he was meant to be collecting. He was rather confused as he climbed back down again.

"Got you!" shouted one of the four policemen who were standing next to the aeroplane's wheels. "Hand over that package laddie. You're going to go down for a very long time."

The Dutch police had worked out what was going on and had allowed the Schiphol maintenance man to position his drugs package before arresting him. They had then rounded up the rest of the gang in Holland. After this, they tipped off the police at Norwich Airport, so it was just a question of waiting for someone to attempt to retrieve the package when the plane landed.

The plan was for them to move in at this point and catch the villain at the English end red-handed. They would then have captured the entire gang and one more group of drug smugglers would face justice. The English police were at as much of a loss as the baggage handler, when no trace could be found of the package. They couldn't arrest him without the drugs as evidence, so had no option but to let him go for the time being.

The former baggage handler left the airport as fast as he possibly could. He obviously didn't understand what had gone wrong, but immediately resolved to give up drug smuggling. In future, he would follow some safer form of employment - like robbing banks.

Back at the car, everyone was mystified as to where the drugs had come from, but as they were unlikely to have been a gift from heaven, they deduced that they must have dropped from a plane.

The pub landlord decided to call Norwich Airport police and returned inside to do so.

"It's certainly made a mess of your car, John," George remarked. "You don't seem to be having a lot of luck with that Jaguar recently."

"I was getting a bit bored with it anyway," John

told him. "I've been thinking lately about changing it and this has just given me the push I needed."

"So what will you buy next?" Tom asked.

"I've been considering getting a Bentley. That way, you lot could really be chauffeured around in style!"

The other three all thought that this sounded like a really good idea to them.

The local policeman turned up on his pushbike to guard the car until the officers from the drugs squad arrived. He wobbled into the car park having just been woken up from his afternoon nap. That extra pint or two he'd drunk at lunchtime had left him muddleheaded and decidedly unsteady on his bike.

The boys returned to their game of petanque as he went and stood by the car, trying hard to look as if he had the situation under control.

When the other policemen finally put in an appearance, they immediately decided that John's Jaguar would need to be impounded, as it was crucial evidence in the case against the smugglers. John simply told them to do what they liked with it.

"I will just arrange to hire another car in the morning," he told the others. "There's no point in me calling out my garage to collect the Jaguar, if the police intend to hang on to it." They removed the rest of their luggage and their personal possessions from the boot of the car, under the watchful eye of a police inspector. There was nothing they needed from the interior which was just as well, as the inspector didn't want anything inside the car disturbed.

It was now early evening and time to think about what they should do with regard to an evening meal. As their options were rather limited in Cawston, they went back into the pub to check out the menu.

18

AN EVENING IN CAWSTON

As they ate their dinner in the pub, they discussed the success of the Cromer weekend. Fred hadn't yet prepared his results sheet, but the rest all knew that it would be the first thing he attended to as soon as he got home. Fred was Mr Reliability when it came to things like that.

"I'm still trying to decide what stands out as the highlight of the weekend," said George. "I can't quite decide between John doing his Clint Eastwood bit in the jewellers, or Tom rescuing Miss Cromer."

"Bear in mind that Tom also caught the golden crab," Fred reminded him. "Not to mention being identified as a lecherous old man in front of the entire audience in the pier theatre."

"I'm not likely to forget that," Tom commented, as he remembered his embarrassment at the time.

"Yes," said John. "We've certainly crammed a lot into the last three days but for me, the highlight has to be delivering that baby. It's true that it wasn't strictly speaking part of the Cromer weekend, but it was an experience none of us are ever likely to forget. We brought a brand new life into this world and didn't even know what we were doing."

It's a shame we ended up having a row with the hotel manager," Fred chipped in, "but he is such a pompous ass and had it coming. He'd been on our backs since the very first time we ever stayed there."

"Are you thinking about that time when we sat at the wrong table?" John asked.

"Yes," said Fred, "There was that, but I was also thinking of the argument about how many eggs I was allowed to have for breakfast."

Tom didn't know what Fred was talking about, as he had been late down to breakfast on the day the incident happened. He asked him to explain.

Fred told him that he had ordered two poached eggs for breakfast, together with a couple of rashers of bacon and a grilled tomato.

"So what's wrong with that?" Tom queried.

"Well," said John. "According to hotel policy, if you order three or more items including an egg, then you are only entitled to a single egg."

"But the price is still the same whatever you order for a cooked breakfast," Tom pointed out, "and the full English includes an egg, two rashers of bacon, a grilled tomato, a sausage, mushrooms and baked beans. That's six items in total. Not to mention that you also get as many slices of toast as you want and can have fruit or cereal to start with, as well as fruit juice and unlimited cups of coffee or tea. That's a hell of a lot more than a couple of eggs, two rashers of bacon and a grilled tomato, so Fred should have been allowed to have his two eggs. "

"Exactly," said Fred, "and that's what I tried to tell the waitress. I said that I fully expected to pay the same price as for the full English, but that I just wanted a lighter breakfast with two eggs."

"So what happened next?" Tom asked.

"She kept insisting that I could only have one egg, so I then offered to pay for the extra egg and asked her how much it would cost."

"What did she say then?" He was now warming to this tale of the hotel's crazy management policies.

"She didn't have an answer to that one," Fred told him. "So she went back into the kitchen to ask for guidance from her boss."

"So did you get your two eggs in the end?"

"I did indeed," continued Fred, "but they were both so overcooked as to be virtually inedible."

"You should have ordered fried eggs instead of poached ones," Tom told him.

"I'd tried that the previous day, but was only given one fried egg instead of the two I'd ordered. That was just as overcooked as the two poached ones I did eventually have served to me."

"Definitely time for a change of hotel," John said. "Let's just hope we don't have any problems like that when we order breakfast here in the morning."

When they had finished their meals, they found seats in the bar and began talking to some of the locals, who by now had begun arriving for a Sunday evening at their local. They were rather surprised to find that news of their midwifery exploits had already spread right round the village and that they were being treated like celebrities. That and the fact that it had been John's car that had been singled out for an aerial assault had made them the men of the moment.

The police had by now covered the Jaguar with a tarpaulin and taken it away on the back of a car transporter. There were still a number of officers in the car park though and they were busy sweeping up the remaining cocaine with brooms and brushes and bagging it up.

"Cleanest I've seen the car park looking in years," the landlord commented, as he watched them finishing off and leaving.

A few minutes later and the new father entered the pub. He was given a rousing cheer by everyone in the place. He looked suitably embarrassed, but then saw the four boys and rushed over to speak to them. "I didn't expect to see you here," he said. "I thought you would be on your way home by now. Please let me buy you a drink, as it is the least I can do after everything you did for me."

Tom glanced down and noticed that the man's shoes and trousers legs were bone dry. "You got the car started and drove here I presume," he asked.

"No," he was told. "The car still won't start, so I walked."

"So how come you didn't get soaked crossing the ford?" Tom queried.

"Oh, I used the old wooden bridge to get across," he was told. "It's just a few yards off the side of the track. Surely I mentioned it to you when you left our cottage to come here to get help?"

"No you didn't," said Tom. "We all waded across the stream in our bare feet!"

"Sorry about that," he said.

They all asked how the baby was doing and were told that mother and baby were fine. The nurse had thoroughly examined both of them when she was there and his wife's sister had now arrived from Cromer and was going to stay with them for a few days.

"That gave me the opportunity to call in here for a drink or two," the husband said. "I really needed one after everything that has happened today."

"You and us both," said John. "We decided to spend the night here and return home in the morning, but then we had a bit more trouble with the Jaguar, so I will now need to hire a car to get us home."

Peter (the new father) hadn't heard anything about the drugs package hitting the car and sat there listening incredulously as the story was related.

"You guys have certainly had to put up with a lot since coming to my assistance," he said. "I'm really sorry for all the problems I've caused you."

"Don't worry about it," John told him. "We've had such an eventful weekend that we're getting used to unexpected things happening to us all the time."

They told Peter something of the highlights of their last three days in Norfolk and he found it hard to believe some of the things they were telling him. He was particularly interested when they mentioned about Tom saving Miss Cromer's life and wanted to hear more about what happened.

"So you're the man who saved Jenny Brown when she was about to plunge down that cliff, are you?" he asked Tom. "I've already been told some of the story, but I didn't know that you chaps were involved."

Four very surprised faces greeted this comment and Tom immediately asked Peter who had told him about the incident.

"Jenny did," he answered. "She's my sister in law and is looking after Mary and the baby at the cottage while I'm here. You will be able to see her again if you do call by in the morning. I'm sure she will be thrilled to hear that the four of you are staying here in the village."

Tom was perplexed to hear this and didn't know whether it was good news or bad. He fully intended to contact Miss Cromer again, but wanted to test the water first by sending her an e-mail or calling her on the phone. He wasn't sure that he was quite ready for a face to face meeting.

"Well, there's a turn up for the books," said

George with a grin. "Looks like you are going to get to meet Jenny again a bit earlier than you thought, Tom."

"What did she have to say about me?" Tom asked cautiously. He didn't know what to expect.

"She described you as her hero," Peter told him, "and said that she can't wait to see you again to show her appreciation."

Tom's beaming smile would have lit up a moonless night. He was ecstatic to hear that Jenny still wanted to see him.

"That's all we need," observed Fred, with a groan. "He's not going to stop going on about Jenny now that he knows that."

Tom was still smiling broadly when he said, "I thought you guys would be happy for me."

"I bet Deirdre won't be all that happy about it," John said.

"Who's Deirdre?" Peter asked, looking at the four of them but not getting an answer.

The man who had been sent to retrieve the cocaine package from the plane wasn't all that happy either. Although the police had let him go at the airport, they found and arrested him again immediately they heard about the missing drugs crash landing in Cawston. He was now in a cell at Norwich police station and his proposed career change to robbing banks would need to be put on hold for a while.

John was right when he said that Deidre wouldn't be happy to hear about Jenny, but what he didn't know was that Deidre was already unhappy. When he had spoken to her on the phone and explained about the car breaking down and the four of them delivering a baby, she was far from convinced that he was telling her the truth. It was such a far-fetched story and she immediately began to get suspicious. She knew that John and Tom were as thick as thieves and it would be just like John to provide Tom with an alibi when he needed one.

She had dialled '1471' after getting the phone call to find out where the call had originated from. John had said that they were calling from the pub at Cawston and when she checked the pub's number on the Internet, she discovered that this part at least was true. As for the rest, she wasn't at all sure.

The more she thought about it, the more she came to the conclusion that Tom was definitely up to no good and that John was covering up for him. She decided that as Cawston was only an hour away by car, she would drive up there in the morning and find out exactly what was going on.

"Heaven help him if he is up to something and I catch him at it," she told herself. She had put up with his womanising for long enough and had decided that it was time she did something about it.

Tom would have been very worried had he known what Deidre was planning, but he was blissfully ignorant of her intentions. At that moment, he was so thrilled at the prospect of meeting a grateful Jenny again, that nothing could spoil his good mood. His wife suddenly turning up unannounced in the morning would certainly deflate his euphoria.

When Peter was about to leave, they told him that they intended to call round to see the family late the following morning. They still needed to arrange a hire car and the nearest place to do this would be the town of Aylsham, about five miles away. The landlord had agreed to drive John over there after breakfast, so he could collect the car himself and then pick the rest of them up at the pub. From there they would visit Peter and Mary and see Jenny again, before heading home.

"Let's just hope there aren't any more surprises waiting in store for us," Tom remarked. "We've all been having a pleasant evening here and that dinner was very good. All I need now is a good night's sleep in a comfortable bed and a hearty breakfast in the morning. I will sleep like a baby, knowing that I will be seeing Jenny and the kid again tomorrow. Apart from one or two painful memories, I really did enjoy the weekend, so life really couldn't really get much better for me at this moment."

"I wonder what other attractions Cawston has to offer on a Sunday evening," said George. They had now spent most of their time at Cawston in the pub and he was wondering whether there were any other interesting places they might visit while they were here. He walked over to one of the locals and asked. When he returned, he had a smile on his face.

"What did he have to say?" John asked.

"He told me that there isn't a lot to do in Cawston at any time of the day or night," George told him. "The residents here have the choice of either sitting down in front of their televisions in the evening, or going to the pub."

"There can't be much on the telly tonight, then," Fred observed, "I can't remember when I last saw a village pub this busy on a Sunday evening."

19

BLOOD MAY FLOW

When they came down to breakfast the following morning, they were asked what they wanted to eat. The landlord's wife was doing the cooking and stood by their table with a pad, as she waited to take their orders.

"How many eggs are we allowed each?" Fred asked.

The landlady gave him a confused look. "If you want an omelette, then I usually use three," she said. "For scrambled I generally use two, but if you only want them boiled, poached or fried, then just tell me how many you want."

"So you don't restrict them depending on what we order?" Fred continued saying.

"Why on earth would I do that?" the landlady asked in obvious puzzlement. "It's your breakfast, so I will serve whatever you want. There's no shortage of eggs in Norfolk and you can see chickens running around wherever you look. You could almost call this place the chicken capital of England."

Fred looked pleased to hear this, but decided to order kippers instead, which she had mentioned was another option. The others asked for breakfasts with eggs, just to see how they would turn out. They needn't have worried though, as they were cooked to perfection. Cooking eggs properly is not rocket science, but appears to be a skill some hotels never quite seem to master.

After breakfast, John went off with the landlord to Aylsham, to hire a car to get them home. The others went and had a look at St Agnes church, as they had been told it was worth visiting.

Jenny in the meantime, was trying to decide what to wear for when Tom arrived. She remembered him saying that he wanted to see more of her, when he had been trying to chat her up in the bookies. "I will show him a lot more of me than he expects," she promised herself.

Peter and Mary hadn't been able to get to Cromer to watch her win the Miss Cromer competition, so she had brought with her the revealing swimsuit she had worn for the beauty pageant. She originally intended just to show it to them, but now she would put it on and give Tom the surprise of his life.

When she came downstairs wearing it, Peter's eyes nearly popped out of his head. "Wow!" he said. "That doesn't leave a lot to the imagination, does it? No wonder you won. Once the judges saw you, they probably didn't notice that there were other girls in the competition."

"I know it's not really the sort of thing to wear on a Monday morning," Jenny said, "but I want to try and look my best for Tom, as I think he deserves that."

"I think it's fair to say that he will be bowled over when he sees you wearing that," Mary commented. "I just hope you don't shock him too much."

At Aylsham, John didn't have any problems hiring a suitable car and was soon driving back to Cawston. The landlord had left him as soon as he'd seen that John was getting everything sorted out.

The boys enjoyed visiting the church and by now had returned to the pub to await John's return. Their luggage was already packed, so just needed to be loaded into whatever car he hired. Tom was on tenterhooks as they waited for him to arrive. He knew that Jenny would now be expecting him to call in and was really excited at the thought of seeing her again. "Thank goodness Deidre is miles away," he said to himself, "as that means there's no chance of her ever finding out what's going on here." He was smugly confident, but had seriously underestimated his wife.

Deidre was nothing like as far away as he thought. Having spent the night thinking about the cock and bull story she had been told, she had convinced herself that Tom was definitely up to no good and had made an early start that morning. She was now well on her way to Cawston in her car.

John finally turned up in a huge Range Rover. He

knew he needed to drive through the ford again, so had made sure that he hired a vehicle designed to do things like that. The boys began loading everything into the car, with Tom hurrying them along all the time. Eventually, everything was ready and they set off towards Peter and Mary's cottage.

They had not been gone more than five minutes, when Deidre drove into the car park. The only other car there belonged to the landlord and there was no sign of John's Jaguar at all. As the pub was shut, she began honking her car's horn to attract someone's attention. After a couple of minutes, the landlord came out of the pub and walked over to where she was parked.

"Can I help you?" he asked. He immediately noticed that she seemed to be in a bit of an agitated state.

"I'm looking for my husband," Deidre told him. "He was supposed to be staying here with some friends last night, but I'm not sure if he actually did."

The landlord told her that four gentlemen had been staying there the previous night, but that they had now checked out. "They are still in the area though," he said, "as I know they were planning on calling in to see Mary and the baby before heading home."

When Deidre heard this, she immediately jumped to the wrong conclusion. This Mary, whoever she was, had to be a girlfriend of Tom's and it sounded as if he had got her pregnant, as there was now also a baby. "So where does this Mary live?" Deidre asked, in a tone that sent a cold shiver down the landlord's back.

When the boys arrived at the cottage, Peter opened the door for them. Mary was sitting in an armchair with her new son, but Jenny was nowhere to be seen. The rest rushed over to have a look at the baby, leaving Tom standing in the middle of the room. He was a bit disappointed, as he had expected Jenny to be there to greet him.

"Jenny's upstairs at the moment," Peter told him. "She will be down in a few minutes." Tom's heart was thumping, as he tried to control his emotions.

Jenny suddenly appeared near the bottom of the stairs and entered the room. You could hear a pin drop as four sets of eyes turned to stare at her. She was wearing the briefest of low cut swimsuits imaginable and had the Miss Cromer crown on her head. She broke the sudden silence by saying, "Hi fellows, I'm pleased to see you all again," before walking straight over to Tom and giving him a great big kiss, "and a special greeting for my hero."

Tom's brain was turning somersaults as she led him over to the sofa and pulled him down to sit next to her. She then put one of her arms around his shoulders and gave him a big squeeze, before kissing him again. The others didn't know what to say, but they were all secretly wishing that they could change places with Tom at that moment. The lucky sod was really revelling in the attention being lavished upon him by the extremely scantily clad Miss Cromer.

There was a ring on the doorbell and Peter got up to answer it. As the front door led directly into the lounge, Deidre could see the entire room as it swung open. She immediately saw Tom sitting on the sofa being cuddled by some girl wearing next to nothing. She also noticed that he had bright red lipstick marks all over his face. Tom's mouth fell open in stunned surprise as Deidre stormed into the room.

"Get your hands off my husband!" she screamed at Jenny.

"He's your husband?" Jenny squealed back, as she leapt to her feet. The very low cut top half of her swimsuit had been defying gravity up until that very moment, but now gave up the struggle and fell away. Both her breasts were suddenly exposed and she frantically tried to cover them, while everyone else in the room was far too stunned to move.

If Tom wasn't right in the middle of having a heart attack at that moment, he was certainly exhibiting all the symptoms. He slumped back on the sofa gasping for air, his face now redder than the lipstick marks.

Jenny ran towards the stairs, but was hampered by the swimsuit, which was now on its way down to her knees. Deidre was across the room in a flash and put an arm lock round the almost naked girl's neck. She would have strangled Jenny but for John and George, who leapt up and grabbed hold of her.

It took all their strength to drag Deidre away, but they finally managed to pull her off and forced her down on the sofa. Jenny stood there shaking for a moment, but then suddenly realised that she was naked and bolted up the stairs.

The commotion woke up the baby and he began to cry loudly. Also at that moment, the telephone rang. BT had finally got around to repairing the line to the house and were ringing to let the owners know.

George was tightly hanging on to Deidre, who had managed to take a swing at Tom while they were trying to get her down on the sofa. He now had a handkerchief to his nose and was attempting to stop the blood flow.

"If we could all just calm down for a minute," John said, "I think I might be able to sort out this mess." He looked directly at Deidre, who was still struggling furiously. "Deidre has understandably jumped to a conclusion based on what she saw when the door was opened. An explanation of what was actually going on might make her see things a bit differently."

"This had better be good," Deidre snarled, but she did stop fighting against George and appeared to be prepared to listen.

John began explaining how everything he had told her on the phone was true and that the car really had broken down, when they were on their way to help deliver Mary's baby. Mary lifted up her son to show him to Deidre.

"So, who is the baby's father?" Deidre demanded.

"I'm his father," said Peter, as he walked across the room to join his wife, "and your husband and his friends came to my assistance, when I couldn't get Mary to the hospital yesterday. They delivered our baby."

"So what has that naked hussy got to do with all this and why was she all over my husband?"

"That naked hussy, as you put it, is Mary's sister," John told her. "Tom saved her life while we were in Cromer. We didn't know that she was here and were very surprised to see her when we arrived. She was in the middle of thanking Tom for saving her when you walked in. She may have been doing it a bit too enthusiastically, but she is still suffering from shock after her accident and is emotionally upset at the moment."

"Even if what you're telling me is true," countered Deidre, "that doesn't explain why she was doing so half naked?"

"I can answer that," said Peter, stepping in to prove that he could spin a yarn just as well as John. "She had been showing Mary and me the costume she wore for the Miss Cromer competition. She was still wearing it when the boys unexpectedly turned up to see how our new son is getting on."

"Oh!" said Deidre, as she suddenly realised that what John and Peter had said did explain what she had seen as she arrived. She wasn't to know that they had both massaged the truth to get Tom off the hook. She now felt that she was the one who had actually caused the problem, by misreading what was apparently a relatively innocent situation.

"I have rather put my foot in it, haven't I?" Deidre stammered. "I can only apologise to you all and hope you will be able to forgive me."

"You will need to apologise to Jenny," said Peter. "I don't know what you would have done to her if the boys hadn't dragged you off when they did."

Deidre didn't know what to say. She had made a complete fool of herself in front of strangers and had violently attacked a young woman who was already emotionally stressed out.

"I will go and get her," said Mary, as she handed her son over to Peter.

Jenny was fully dressed when she came down and understandably rather nervous about having to face Deidre again. She listened as she apologised, but then looked really shocked when Deidre told her that she had suspected Tom and her of having an affair.

"I find it hard to believe that you could possibly think that," she said to Deidre. "Just look at me and then look at your husband. He's old enough to be my grandfather. Why on earth would I want to get involved with him?"

The boys fell about laughing and Tom realised that his days of chasing women were well and truly over. He had thought that despite his age, Jenny really did have some feelings for him, but all his hopes were now dashed. He looked totally dejected.

As they all went back to the two cars some time

later, Jenny said she wanted a word with Tom before he left. He stayed behind as the rest went outside. When there was just the two of them, Jenny partly closed the door and threw her arms round his neck. She kissed him passionately and when they both came up for air, she spoke, "I didn't mean a single word I said back there, but had to say something like that because your wife was so suspicious. I can't wait for you to come and see me again and the next time we meet, I really will show you how grateful I can be."

It was only with the greatest effort that Tom managed to stop himself leaping for joy as he went and joined Deidre in the car. They would drive home together, while the others all went with John in the Range Rover. He felt a bit guilty about Deidre being conned into believing him to be innocent, but he would enjoy her trying to make up for doubting him.

The boy's weekend was now over and it was time to go home. Without a doubt, it had been the best one ever and Tom's luck did appear to have finally changed, as he had always known it would. He was looking forward to telling the others what Jenny had said to him, but that would have to wait until they were all together again in the Nag's Head and Deidre was nowhere around.

EPILOGUE

Some readers may feel outraged that Tom managed to get away with it, but did he? More of that later ...

When John's Jaguar was taken to be investigated at the forensic laboratory, there was a slip up on the paperwork that went with it. Someone had stated that the car needed to be examined for drugs, when they should have said that the drugs in the car needed to be examined. As a result, the enthusiasts there tore the car apart, looking for more cocaine concealed within it. By the time they had stripped it down to a basic shell, having ripped the interior to pieces, John's Jaguar was only fit for the scrap yard.

It was a very apologetic chief inspector who rang John to give him the news. He told him that there would be no need for John to contact his insurance company, as the police would pay for the total cost of replacing the Jaguar at its full market value. A cheque would be issued to him within a month.

On the boys first day at Cromer, an argument had broken out at the bowls club, after John had driven his golf ball into the middle of their league game. It was finally resolved when the decision was made to replay the final end. On this occasion, no other golf balls interrupted play and the Sherringham District League players won the final end. This gave them the match and they returned home victorious.

The thieves who had stolen the Jaguar's wheels did not remain at large for very long. The police were able to identify two of the gang from the CCTV images and when they raided one of the addresses they had, they caught the four of them all busy unloading stolen car parts from the back of their van. They were arrested and will soon face justice.

Cromer Council e-mailed Tom to tell him that the crab he had caught was indeed the golden crab and that he had won the competition. The prize was to be an all expenses paid week's holiday for two at the Hotel Splendide (God's waiting room). Tom was not overjoyed to hear this, particularly as Deidre also saw the e-mail. She was over the moon though, as it meant that the two of them could go to Cromer together and she would get to see some of the places the boys frequented on their weekends there.

The other part of the prize was a champagne and lobster dinner at one of Cromer's top restaurants, as the guests of Miss Cromer. After which they would be taken to see a show at the Pavilion Theatre on the pier. Deidre was especially pleased about this, as it would give her another opportunity to apologise to Jenny. Tom was totally distraught. His plans for an evening out with Miss Cromer most certainly didn't include Deidre coming along as well.

The two young men who tried to rob the jewellery shop were both charged with attempted robbery and being in possession of offensive weapons. They will soon have their day in court. As nothing was actually taken, the owner of the store was not overly generous when it came to rewarding the boys for preventing the crime. He sent them each a £25.00 gift voucher, which could only be spent in his shop.

The reporters who had hoped for a scoop to make them famous were also disappointed. Their editor's opinion was that an attempted crime where nothing was actually stolen was not all that newsworthy. They had been expecting a big splash feature article, but all that got was a short paragraph on Page 7, where hardly anyone even noticed it.

The End of the Pier Show finished its run shortly after the boys left, as they had caught one of the last few shows of the season. The good news is that it will be on again next year.

The old couple at the hotel reported Tom to the police for peeing in the street, after the boys had all leered at them at breakfast that morning. They were intent on making trouble for him, but didn't realise that Tom was already known to the police at Cromer, as one of the men who had helped foil the jewellery store robbery the previous night.

The sergeant who interviewed them said that things like that do sometimes happen to a man with prostate problems and suggested that they should find better things to do with their time, rather than wasting his by reporting such trivial incidents. As they left the police station, the colostomy pouch the man carried inside his trousers burst and its contents ran down his leg and onto the pavement. The police promptly arrested him for urinating in the street outside the police station.

The hotel manager didn't know that when he was busy haranguing the boys at breakfast, after having listened to the old couple, that an undercover hotel inspector was also in the breakfast room at the same time. The inspector reported him to the hotel's owners and as this wasn't the first complaint they had received about this manager, they decided to sack him and put someone else in his place.

The smugglers, who had thought they were on to a winner by concealing their drug consignments in the undercarriage spaces on aircraft, discovered that the police had been watching them for some time. There was now more than enough evidence to prosecute them, so they were sent to trial. The only charge that they managed to beat was the one for littering, as the judge couldn't find any legal justification for the littering from a moving aircraft charge, as they weren't actually on the flight at the time. They were however found guilty on every other charge and will now have to face lengthy prison sentences.

John was actually right when he said that Jenny was still in a state of shock after her accident and too emotionally upset to think logically. Reality dawned on her a few days later, when she realised that she had been wantonly throwing herself at an older man and had effectively been promising him goodness knows what. She felt quite disgusted at the thought of what might have happened. It had been a close thing, but she was now thinking rationally again. Tom would need to be told, but she would try and tell him gently. He had saved her life after all.

Peter and Mary, together with John Frederick Thomas George Mulligan are all doing very well and John is due to be christened shortly. The boys have of course been invited to the christening.

When John received the cheque from the police, he went straight to his nearest Bentley dealership and put the money down as the deposit on a nearly new convertible. He thought the boys would enjoy being chauffeured around with the hood down.

Tom finally did get everything he deserved. The numbers on Deidre's lucky dip lottery ticket came up and she won the jackpot. The first he knew about this was when he came home to find her standing there with all her suitcases packed. As she walked out of the front door for the last time, she turned and told him that he would be hearing from her solicitor very shortly, as she was suing him for a divorce on the grounds of his infidelity.

Jenny had called to speak to Tom, but got Deidre instead. She was still feeling guilty about lying to her, so Jenny told Deidre how Tom had responded to her passionate advances with wild enthusiasm and how he had said that he was very much looking forward to further exploring her other charms (she actually used his own words). After she had finished speaking to Jenny, Deidre called her solicitor and instructed him to begin divorce proceedings. She could afford it now.

FRED'S RESULTS SHEET

Putting	George and Fred won by 2 holes
Petanque	Fred & Tom won – 11 to 9
Owzthat	George won with 406 runs. Tom had 397, Fred - 287 and John - 127
Pitch & Putt	Tom & John won. 3 ahead with 2 holes left to play
Team Pool	Fred & John won. 3 out of 5
Football	John won with 5 correct predictions at higher odds than Tom's 5 (George had 4 correct and Fred had 3)
Crazy Golf	Tom & George declared the winners (Match abandoned after 8 holes)
Singles Pool	Fred won a total of 3 games. George won 2 and John won 1. Tom didn't win any at all (the last 3 matches were played out at the Nag's Head)
Points	George - 3pts (2 as a team member) John - 3 pts (2 as a team member) Tom - 3 pts (all as a team member) Fred - 4 pts (3 as a team member)

After considerable discussion, the decision was made to award Tom 2 additional points - one for catching the golden crab and one for saving Miss Cromer's life. This gave him a total of 5 points and the most overall. This made him the weekend's champion, but he was ultimately the loser, as Deidre was the real winner.

ABOUT THE AUTHOR

Mike Turvil is a retired pension consultant, who lives with his wife in Suffolk. He studied at Hampton Grammar School in Middlesex and left there in the early sixties to pursue a number of different careers before becoming a financial adviser. He has varied interests, including model making and cookery, and enjoys a wide range of different types of books. The inspiration to write his own stories came from reading authors such as Douglas Adams and Terry Pratchett many years ago and he likes to try and capture some of their off-beat humour in his own writing.

His books are fun adventures, with plenty of surprises and humour thrown in. Adults should enjoy reading his children's stories every bit as much as their kids, as they will find themselves chuckling at some of the amusing events and impossibly daft situations Mike creates.

FIDO'S TALE

by Mike Turvil

Fido's Tale is a fantasy adventure which will have you laughing out loud. It is an enjoyable romp through prehistory with Fido, a teenage boy who grew up in a dog pack, and a neurotic computer with plans for universal domination.

You will meet a monster crocodile and a crafty old conman - as well as an Egyptian princess and a galactic swarm of giant killer fleas. There is even a pathologically depressed pterodactyl, who wants to be turned into a fire-breathing dragon.

The author weaves a number of historical facts into this imaginative work of fiction, in which one amusing situation leads to the next, but this turns into a roller-coaster ride, as you race towards the story's totally unexpected dramatic climax.

Now available worldwide on Amazon, as both a paperback and a Kindle version.

FIDO: A TWIST IN THE TALE

by Mike Turvil

Having time-travelled to the year 2003, Fido and Nefertari find themselves trapped in a futuristic world. Everything is really strange to them, but they will have to learn fast if they are to survive. Everyday things that we take for granted confuse them and as they don't understand a lot of what they see, they manage to create havoc wherever they go.

Laughter all the way, as we are shown our world through the eyes of a couple from prehistory. There is plenty of excitement as well, as they have to stay ahead of the nationwide police search for them. It will take all of Fido's ingenuity to escape the clutches of the law.

Events occurring in the past add a time dimension to this intriguing story, which switches direction when you least expect it and will catch the unwary by surprise. But you have to expect a challenge, if you are ever to unravel the twist in the tale.

Now available worldwide on Amazon, as both a paperback and a Kindle version.

WILBUR'S QUEST: THE LAST DODO

by Mike Turvil

Wilbur is very unhappy when he discovers he is probably the last dodo, but help is at hand. He meets Horatio and together they set off on a quest to find other dodos.

Their journey takes them round the world, with all its unexpected dangers and excitement. Many problems need to be overcome and Wilbur has to find his hidden strengths in order to survive. But he learns the true meaning of friendship and discovers that nothing is impossible if you have belief in yourself.

Wilbur's Quest is packed full of surprises, but is a really fun adventure story with a message for young readers everywhere.

Will Wilbur's search be successful, or does fate have other plans for him? And what really did happen to the dodos? The history books tell us they became extinct in the seventeenth century, but as they don't mention Wilbur, there is every chance that they might be wrong!

Now available worldwide on Amazon, as both a paperback and a Kindle version.

THE SHED
AT THE BOTTOM OF THE GARDEN

by Mike Turvil

The story of the creatures that live in a typical English garden shed - and their ongoing battle of wits with the man who owns the garden, as well as with his pet dog ("Fearless Freddie"). There are tales of adventure, tales of bravery and tales of love. Over and above everything else, the shed creatures are all dedicated to a common cause; their fight for survival.

A fun-filled romp around the garden, with heroes and baddies. Laughter all the way, as you follow their individual stories. Learn about the broom from above and discover what happened when the bat caught a cold. Feel for the hedgehog that missed having fleas and take part in one of the battles of the aphid wars.

A book to challenge what you might think goes on in the shed at the bottom of your garden.

Now available worldwide on Amazon, as both a paperback and a Kindle version.

21466840R00122

Printed in Poland
by Amazon Fulfillment
Poland Sp. z o.o., Wrocław